The Stephens Children
and
The Scarlet Queen

To Pattie, my soul
To Ian, my spirit

The Stephens Children
and
The Scarlet Queen

S. H. Holloway

'Up the airy mountain' on pages 17–18 is taken from 'The Fairies' by William Allingham

First published in the United Kingdom in 2008
by Publish Me Ltd

You can buy this book directly from the publisher.
Email scarletqueen@sky.com

All the characters in this book are fictitious and any resemblance to real persons, living or dead, is entirely coincidental.

ISBN 978-0-9561033-0-7

Produced by
The Choir Press
www.thechoirpress.co.uk

CHAPTER 1

Gemma Descends
The Stairs

He was dressed all in fur, from his head to his foot,
And his clothes were all tarnished with ashes and soot;
A bundle of toys he had flung on his back,
And he looked like a peddler just opening his pack.

His eyes – how they twinkled! His dimples how merry!
His cheeks were like roses, his nose like a cherry!
His droll little mouth was drawn up like a bow,
And the beard of his chin was as white as the snow.

The stump of a pipe he held tight in his teeth,
And the smoke it encircled his head like a wreath;
He had a broad face and a little round belly,
That shook, when he laughed like a bowlful of jelly!

He was chubby and plump, a right jolly old elf ...

Clement Clark Moore
1823

The sky was midnight blue as the snowflakes spiralled down to the soft white blanket below. The children stared long and hard out of the window as the magical poem was read, their thoughts and dreams lost in a whirl of excitement and anticipation.

Lorna, Christian and Gemma Stephens were staying with Uncle Nicholas in his old rambling Victorian vicarage. He lived in a vicarage because he was the vicar of the village church. During term-time the children were boarders at Drowbridge School, but they had been sent to the vicarage for Christmas as their mother had been admitted to a sanatorium because her thoughts got muddled easily and their father had died many years before but wasn't talked about much. Uncle Nicholas's house was very large, sombre and old fashioned with high ceilings and oak panelling, and threadbare rugs which partially covered gnarled, rugged floorboards tired with use and age. The electricity didn't always work due to the fibrous, twisted, bare wiring, so candles lit most of the rooms and a huge log fire heated the cavernous book-filled study. Uncle Nicholas had a housekeeper called Betty, who was excellent at making hearty broths and sumptuous cakes out of scraps of food conjured up from a few ingredients in the house, but not very good at cleaning so the surfaces were always dusty. You could run your hands along a sideboard leaving long, squiggly lines and draw smiley faces leaving you with black fingertips, especially scorned upon by Betty which showed up her failure.

Some folk in the village said vicar Nicholas was born into a wealthy family but turned his back on the money and gave it all away to needy causes, deciding to join the Ministry instead and preach goodwill to all people in the Church. Whilst he spoke with a 'well-to-do accent' there was no other outward appearance of his monied background. In fact, he didn't even possess a razor or a comb, preferring to leave his white hair tousled and beard casual and unkempt. He always wore a faded sage-green, full-length smoking jacket (but he didn't smoke) with a shabby black fur collar which was thick round his neck and tapered down at his waist. However, despite his dishevelled appearance, he was a very likeable old man and always talked kindly and softly to the children and was as generous as he could be considering his pecuniary status.

The children had not had much time to explore the house as they had only arrived at the vicarage that day. Their minds were preoccupied with the fact that it was Christmas Eve and they were eagerly awaiting the impending visit of Santa Claus. Gemma, the youngest girl (aged ten) and the one with the most inquisitive manner, asked first.

'Lorna, do you think you've been good enough to receive a present from Santa Claus this year?'

Lorna (aged fifteen) made no hesitation in her reply, saying, 'Of course I have, but we all know who hasn't ...', turning round to face Christian with that very serious, knowledgeable expression of hers.

Christian (aged thirteen and unlucky for some) retaliated swiftly to the comment with immediate anxiety and concern, saying, 'It wasn't my fault, how did I know that the ice was that thin and *he* would do the dare?'

'Yes, but you didn't need to laugh as well,' Lorna quickly pointed out. 'He could have died of pneumonia and his mother wouldn't have been too happy about that.'

'Now children, enough of that bickering, the main thing is that Christian has learned his lesson and hopefully won't do such a mischievous thing again ... will you Christian?' said Uncle Nicholas, holding the last three words of his sentence in the air for a few moments for controlling effect, whilst peering over his bifocals anxiously at him. Christian shrank back on the stool coyly and it was quite evident that whether he got a present from Santa Claus or not was now out of his hands.

With a clap of his hands, Uncle Nicholas ordered, 'Up to bed now all of you and try to sleep, no peeping until at least six in the morning.'

The children slid off their stools and pottered slowly out into the hallway. Gemma lagged behind and when the other two had gone up the creaky staircase, she turned to the well-built man standing tall above her and said, 'Uncle Nicholas, do you think Mummy will ever be well? I would love to see her again.'

The man gave a gentle half smile and replied, 'I think she will,' tapping her on her shoulder reassuringly whilst guiding her towards the door. Out in the huge, dark hallway, Gemma rested her back against the solid oak study door and pondered momentarily.

'Psst!' resounded through the void. 'Psst, over here ...' Gemma looked round and down and her eyes set upon a rather rotund, larger than normal mouse wearing brown calico dungarees, a fawn-coloured shirt and a flat cap perched on his head above his protruding ears. The mouse was standing upright and leaning against the panel supporting the stairs. Beckoning with his index finger he said, 'Come over here and follow me.' The mouse turned his back to Gemma and faced the panel, walked straight at it and disappeared. Stunned, but hugely curious, Gemma walked up to where the mouse had been and cautiously raised her hand to the panel, expecting to hit the wood. To her surprise she didn't, and she toppled forward falling flat on the cold ground below her feet.

When she pulled herself up from the floor and looked up, she was surrounded by complete blackness except for a small candle lighting a set of spiral stairs in front of her. On the top stair stood the mouse with a cheery expression. 'I'm Morsel, Morsel by name, Morsel by nature. Don't need to tell me yours, we've been expecting you, Lorna and Christian. Pleased to meet you.'

Still in a state of semi-shock, Gemma blurted out, 'And you too ... Mr M ... Morsel.' Morsel marched off down the stairs clearly with the intent of Gemma following him, which she dutifully did. She should have been more cautious but curiosity had got the better of her. As they descended, the light gradually started to increase and the faint sound of a tapping noise transcended the air around them. The steps seemed endless, in fact there were 998 of them, but the light before them got brighter and brighter, the clanking noise louder and louder and Gemma seemed to get dizzier and dizzier as they approached the bottom.

A massive wooden door, framed by light and mechanical noises, confronted them. As before, Morsel walked straight through it and Gemma followed with much more ease and confidence than her previous experience upstairs. She remained upright but her jaw dropped open as she surveyed the wondrous sight before her eyes.

CHAPTER 2

What Gemma Found There

'Welcome, Gemma,' echoed the chorus.

'How lovely to meet you,' came a distinctly solitary Scottish voice beside her. She turned as she was greeted by the rather husky tone. He was only a little smaller than herself and wore a full-length green coat with red and blue tartan pockets, held closed by a rather wide black belt with a great big silver buckle. He was similar to a man, but different. His ears were pointed at both the top and the bottom and were disproportionately large for his head. His hair stopped short of his shoulders and was very dark grey, which coincidentally matched his triangular shaped beard. He resembled the human form, but as Gemma had read many books she instantly knew that he was a dwarf. 'Hello,' he chirped, 'I'm Haggis,' which Gemma didn't find terribly surprising as he had a Scottish accent – not that all dwarves from Scotland should be called Haggis. However, he continued, 'Where are the other Angels?'

'What other *Angels*?' enquired Gemma.

'Lorna and Christian,' replied Haggis.

'Oh they're not angels, well, in fact, nor am I. But I would say that Lorna is more of an angel than Christian, she's always the good one, and the most intelligent. Anyway, they've gone to bed.'

'Gone to bed tonight?' asked Haggis with much astonishment. 'But we were expecting them, too.'

This was something that had been puzzling Gemma. 'Just why are you expecting us?' she asked, displaying her normal inquisitive facial expression.

11

'Don't you know?' replied Haggis. 'After all, that's why you are staying with your uncle Nicholas isn't it?'

'Well, not exactly ... it's because our mother is ...' she tailed off and screwed up her mouth with even more puzzlement.

Gemma decided then that the wider scene in front of her needed much more attention. The room she was in was an enormous workshop, full of various creatures busy doing things with happy, smiling faces and jolly attitudes. The occupants were in groups – more dwarves to the right-hand side and fairies to the left-hand side. The dwarves were much smaller than Haggis, all wearing green waistcoats, with tartan pockets and wide black belts adorned with silver buckles. Their hair was also the same style as Haggis's, but their bodies were all shapes and sizes – some very tall and thin, some very small and fat and some just what she would call normal. Gemma had also spotted the fairies and her slight distraction was interrupted by Haggis's announcement: 'The fairies are all very colourful you know, they are known as the "Rainbow Fairies".' The fairies were all shapes and sizes too, but they had different brightly coloured dresses. The words of the rainbow song sprang to Gemma's mind – 'Pink and yellow and green and blue, orange and purple and . . .', well something like that . . .

With an uncharacteristically authoritative approach, Gemma decided she really ought to establish why such importance was being placed upon not only her visit, but the visit of her brother and sister as well. 'Why exactly are you expecting us?' she asked.

'You are going to help us,' replied Haggis.

'Help you? . . . But I can't sew and I certainly can't make wooden toys. Nor can Lorna and Christian. Lorna reads a lot and is very clever and Christian gets up to all sorts of pranks and is very naughty and I, I just make up stories and poems and like acting.'

'Precisely. That's precisely why you Angels have been sent to us. With your talents, we can overthrow the Scarlet Queen. Otherwise we cannot get around this Christmas Eve and deliver all our presents to the children, and just think of their disappointment!' It was at this point that Gemma realised that she must be in something like Santa's Grotto.

'Well, I can quite see that,' said Gemma, failing to focus on the seriousness of dealing with the Scarlet Queen bit.

'You see, the Scarlet Queen is an evil woman – she makes it darkness all the time so that the children here never see daylight and can never come out to play. She controls the whole of Outlands, ruling it with a rod of iron and venomous fear. The menfolk toil for eighteen hours a day in her coal mines or chop logs in Tall Tree Forest for barely enough money to feed and clothe their families. She uses the coal and logs to burn in her many enormous fires in and around her palace and her workers receive only a lump of coal a week, not enough to keep their families warm. The wives work as servants in her palace and also work such long, tiring hours that they hardly spend any waking time with their infants. The children have no fun or enjoyment and are often ill due to malnutrition and cold. All year round we make toys to take round for the children on Christmas Eve, but this year the Scarlet Queen has issued a "*Royal Puritan Decree, the Queen's Command*" ordering us not to deliver them. We still will though because we know those poor sad children need our help.'

'Oh, how dreadful,' gasped Gemma. 'Those poor children, what a horrid Queen, does she really hate happiness that much?'

'Apparently so,' replied Haggis, shaking his head very sorrowfully. 'She worships ultimate power over good and there is nothing we can do to prevent her wickedness.'

'But what on earth can *we* do in this situation?' Gemma enquired with a very bemused expression,

'If the fires go out, she loses her power and she has no energy to function without heat – that's where you can help.'

'I'm really not altogether sure about this,' responded Gemma with a very high degree of hesitation. 'I don't think Uncle Nicholas would want us to get involved with anything like this. After all, fire is very dangerous you know, Haggis. Anyway, why can't the dwarves and fairies do this?'

With a shrug of his green shoulders Haggis replied, 'They can't go out. As soon as they step out of the door the Scarlet Queen's warthogs will smell them and send word back to the palace, and she will send her winged wolves out to eat them.'

At this, the dwarves all looked up and chirped into spontaneous song. The fairies stopped work and listened. It was a sort of a poem, but set to some quite jolly, catchy music:

'Up the airy mountain
down the rushy glen,
we daren't go a-hunting
for fear of little men;
Wee folk, good folk,
trooping all together
Green Jacket, red cap
and white owl's feather!

'Down along the rocky shore
Some make their home,
They live on crispy pancakes
Of yellow tide-foam;
Some in the reeds
Of the black mountain lake,
With frogs for their watch-dogs,
All night awake.

'By the craggy hill-side,
Through the mosses bare,
They have planted thorn-trees
For pleasure here and there.
Is any man so daring
As dig them up in spite,
He shall find their sharpest thorns
In his bed at night.

'Up the airy mountain
down the rushy glen,
we daren't go a-hunting
for fear of little men;
Wee folk, good folk,
trooping all together
Green Jacket, red cap
and white owl's feather!'

At the end of the song, the fairies went back to sewing feathers on the clothes of the dolls and the dwarves to chiselling the shapes of wooden soldiers and trains.

'My word,' gasped Gemma, 'how frightfully awful. You don't want that do you?' she exclaimed in a rhetorical question-like approach. 'But wouldn't they smell us and eat us too?' she asked in a quizzical manner.

'No, no, you are of earth blood and the souls of heaven and here you would not heat up enough for the scent to be noticed, unless you have a cut and your blood flows out. You are also watched over by the Father of All Angels, being of that family protection. Santa Claus protects us, but he had his energy drained the day that the Scarlet Queen arrived in Outlands. The good and the evil cannot live harmoniously together.'

Gemma had listened to Haggis and wondered what to say.

'Please, you have to help us – the children of Outlands need you . . . we need you. Please go and fetch Lorna and Christian and come back as quickly as possible so that we can plan what to do.'

Spontaneously Gemma followed Morsel and ran back up the 998 steps as though there were only nine. Breathless at the top, she paused, thanked Morsel and walked back through the under-stairs panel. Back in the comfort of the Vicarage, she leaned against the hallway wall and thought. She could hear that Uncle Nicholas was still in his study reading but she decided not to worry him with her experience and promptly headed up to bed as she had been away for ages.

CHAPTER 3

What To Do Next?

Gemma was exceedingly excited and at the same time terribly scared. She didn't really know what to do, but she knew she had to do something. It was all so bizarre, so strange and she knew no-one would believe her. Perhaps it had been a dream, perhaps she had fainted and the whole thing was a figment of her imagination. She yawned as she was extremely tired but she couldn't sleep.

As she reluctantly slipped into bed, Lorna spoke. 'Where have you been for the past ten minutes?'

'Ten minutes, what do you mean ten

minutes? I've been gone for a very long while,' replied Gemma.

'Don't be so silly, only enough time to get lost, find the bathroom and clean your teeth,' responded Lorna in her usual frank way.

In frustration and annoyance at Lorna Gemma clenched the palms of her hands and realised that in her left hand she was holding something soft and gentle yet framed on a rigid backbone. It was a pure white feather, one of the feathers that the fairies had been sewing onto the dolls' dresses. Gemma leapt up from the bed like a spring. 'Don't say that. I've been somewhere very, very special. I've been to Santa Claus's Grotto where they make all the toys and games for the children and they desperately need our help as the Scarlet Queen is going to stop them delivering tonight . . .' Gemma tailed off breathlessly.

'You're in your own little make-believe world again,' said Lorna with her normal tone of indignation. To be fair, Gemma did make up stories, but only for the purposes of self-entertainment so it is understandable that Lorna thought this was just another one. However, we know that this one wasn't, but Gemma was going to have to convince her siblings that it was the truth.

'No seriously, something really did happen, I'll go and fetch Christian and tell you both together,' gushed Gemma as she disappeared out of the room. As most boys are when asleep, Christian was dead to the world and she struggled to waken him. She shook him, pulled his arm and shrieked in his ear. Finally he stirred, his waking words being, 'What has Santa Claus brought me?'

'Nothing, silly, it's still only nine o'clock and he won't bring you anything unless we help him,' blurted Gemma.

'Don't call me "silly", you're the silly one wittering on about helping Santa Claus,' replied Christian. 'Anyway I really don't believe in him and nor does Lorna. We didn't say before because you're too young to tell yet . . .' At which point Lorna entered the room and heard the end of Christian's sentence.

'I have to say Gemma, Christian is right. Santa Claus doesn't exist and the presents we received on Christmas Eve were really given to us by Mother. I am sorry to disappoint you but you need to put a stop to your nonsense and we need to get to sleep or else we won't get any presents at all,' commanded Lorna.

'It's so not nonsense,' cried Gemma. 'Look, here's a feather which I got from the Grotto that proves it.' Lorna studied the feather but Christian had no interest, preferring to go back to sleep, and wished the girls would go away.

'Please, please listen. It's so important and really is the truth.' Gemma had pleaded so earnestly that Lorna decided to question her a little more. All she wanted was to disprove her fairytale so that they could all get back to bed.

'If we are to believe your fairytale, where is Santa's Grotto?' she enquired.

'It's under the stairs,' replied Gemma.

Lorna smiled. 'Under the stairs?' she repeated. 'Yes, I can see it as a room, in fact a very, very, very small room more likely to house a vacuum cleaner, an ironing board, a mop and bucket and a duster ... and not really very much more,' she said, nodding and smiling with sympathy.

'No you don't understand, it leads to a spiral staircase of nine hundred and ninety eight steps down to the Grotto,' insisted an exasperated Gemma.

Lorna couldn't help but giggle, saying, 'Now I do know you are slightly puddled. Come to bed and you'll have forgotten your daydream in the morning and then we can open our presents.'

Almost at full volume, Gemma shouted, 'There won't be any presents unless you believe me!'

Lorna sensed that Gemma would not settle until there was some way of placating her. So she gave Christian a nudge in the ribs and in a very patronising way said, 'Come on Christian, let's all go and see Santa's Grotto in the under-stairs cupboard,' as she nudged his elbow and winked at him.

Therefore the three quietly crept down the stairs and into the very dark, cold hallway. Uncle Nicholas had gone to bed and the study door was ajar showing the room was pitch black and unoccupied. Gemma led the way to the under-stairs panel where she had gone through earlier and stood in front of it.

'This is it, you just walk through it,' informed Gemma. Christian nearly fell to his knees with mirth and Lorna looked towards the ceiling with despair.

'Now you are joking,' chuckled Christian. 'Go on, Houdini, after you!'

'Just watch,' remonstrated Gemma, who promptly walked straight into the solid panel and banged her head. Christian burst out laughing and Lorna struggled to keep a straight face.

'I think we can now safely say that it's all a bit of a ruse, Gemma, and that the feather tricked us for a while, but it really came out of one of your pillows. However, we must get back to bed, come on.'

Crestfallen and humiliated, Gemma trundled back across the hallway after the other two with a heavy heart. She hadn't made it up – it had really happened.

'Psst!' once again resounded through the void. 'Psst, over here, hurry, hurry, hurry, the Rainbow Fairies have been kidnapped . . .' This time they all looked round and their eyes set upon the rather rotund, larger than normal mouse wearing brown calico dungarees, standing upright and leaning against the panel supporting the stairs. Again, beckoning with his crooked index finger he said, 'Come over here and follow me.' The mouse turned his back to the children, faced the panel, walked straight at it and disappeared. This time, the two disbelieving jaws dropped and their owners stood motionless.

'That's Morsel,' enthused Gemma. 'Quick, we must follow him, the whole thing has started.'

Now of course we all know that Lorna was going to take the sensible, cautious approach and it was no surprise that she was going to say, 'You must be joking, we can't possibly do that. This is the maddest thing possible, we don't know who *he* is; what *he's* got in mind and where *he's* taking us. We'd be absolutely barmy to follow him, and what would Uncle Nicholas say if we never returned?'

However, we also now all know that Christian would never have taken the sensible, cautious approach and was always going to be most reckless in his behaviour. Grabbing both Lorna and Gemma by the arms he cried like a banshee, 'Come on, the adventure starts here!' As a result, they all bolted through the panel with such force that they ended up on top of each other with Morsel underneath. Morsel extricated himself from the base of the bundle, shook himself and dusted off his clothing.

When he had regained his composure he cleared his throat and said, 'Welcome, although I hadn't expected quite such a notable entrance. However we must make haste as time is ticking on and we've now only got the dwarves to fill Santa's sleigh. We must find the fairies soon, or she'll feed them to the horrid winged wolves.'

They got to the bottom of the stairs in no more than seconds, as though they had glided down. Yet again, they all ended up in a heap, thankfully with Christian at the base this time. As they peered in front of them, two huge, black leather lumps confronted them and an enormous, jolly 'Ho, ho, ho,' echoed through the air.

CHAPTER 4

The Rainbow Fairies

'Get off my frock, you horrid little vermin!' yelled Petal in the pink dress.

'Take your paws off me, you poor apology for a creature,' mocked Buttercup in the yellow dress.

'Watch where you're sticking that, you rancid rat!' shrieked Fern in the emerald dress.

'What a cheek, you smelly, grotesque thing!' screamed Bluebell in the blue dress.

More inquisitive Poppy in the tangerine dress enquired, 'Where are we?'

'What are you going to do with us?' asked Iris in the purple dress.

All of the fairies were dressed in very vivid and bright dresses, resembling colours of the rainbow, hence their names. They wore make-up and had their hair arranged in various different styles and took great pride in their appearance.

Both of the rats were really horrible looking and one was fat and the other was thin. In addition, both of them were ignorant and unintelligent. The fairies quickly realised this as they were fairly clever.

All six of them were huddled in the corner of a very dark, dank, dreary cell with water dripping off the cold, solid stone walls. The two miserable, dishevelled grey rats stood guard at the door, leaning on rusty muskets and drinking ale from metal mugs as they watched the fairies try to brush out the creases of their skirts and attempt to put their messed-up hair back into place.

Addressing one of the morons, Buttercup asked, 'Don't suppose there's a mirror anywhere here?'

'Oh yes, and a hairbrush,' added Poppy.

One of the rats spat his ale back out of his mouth with mirth, whilst the other bent double with laughter and fell over his musket. 'We should have a bit of fun here with this lot,' giggled one of them.

'Yes, by the time we've finished with them, they won't know a perm from a bouffant,' said the other, rocking with glee. In a vain attempt, the fairies continued to tidy their apparel, but it was hopeless.

'If we hadn't been bundled into the back of that ghastly, filthy cart, we wouldn't look like we do now – it's all your fault, look at my shoes, they've got water marks from the rain,' wailed Bluebell.

'Shut up and stop moaning,' shouted one of the rats, 'or else you will know what it's like to get very wet, ha ha—'

With no announcement (nor warning) the huge wooden cell door flung open with such noise and force that it sent the two rats crashing against the side cell wall, where they hung in the air momentarily and then slithered to the stone floor in a pile on top of each other. Suddenly a rumble reverberated through the cell and the fairies pinned themselves against the rear wall in terror, the apparition ahead both breathtaking and bewildering. A booming voice was accompanied by a vista of red and black – a woman had entered. She was about seven foot tall, thin as a rake with one half of her head covered with jet-black hair and the other with crimson-coloured hair piled up in a bun and held down with a long hat pin with a big ruby on the end of it. Her face was stern and her features pointed; large black eyes and red-coated lips punctuated her ashen complexion. Her dangly earrings matched her hat pin and glistened like fire as she swayed her head to and fro in a commanding fashion. She wore a full-length scarlet robe completely shaped to her body with a bird-wing type collar and wide black belt held in place by yet another enormous ruby clasp, which smouldered as she gyrated in animated movement. The vision was awesome.

Behind her were three ugly wizened witches: one was tall and thin; one was short and fat; and the other was quite simply grotesque. They all had crooked noses and pasty lips. They twisted and wrung their scrawny hands in excitement.

'Excellent, excellent,' she spoke. 'Get up, you silly little rats and make sure these fairies endure as much discomfort as possible before we decide their fate.' The rats raised themselves from the ground in eager anticipation. The Queen swept across the cell towards the fairies, towering above them, and poked Petal in the chest. 'Wonderful, I've got you now, those *happy humans* will have to come and find you and then I will capture and torment them too. Christmas will no longer exist and I will rule Outlands with prohibition, misery, poverty and sadness. My *Royal Puritan*

Decree, the Queen's Command will be enforced ... let the plan commence ...' She spun round and swirled back out of the door. The door slammed behind her and the cell fell silent.

After a few minutes, Petal took courage and asked, 'Who was *that*?'

With utter dismay and snivelling loyalty, one of the rats responded, *'That's* the Scarlet Queen, the ruler of Outlands and one who must be feared.'

'What an outfit, wonder where she got that one from?' quizzed Bluebell.

'And her hair ... quite amazing,' added Fern.

'Wonder what she wants with us?' sensibly enquired Poppy.

'We've got to get out of here,' pleaded Buttercup.

'Hear, hear!' cried Petal, who started tapping at the walls of the dungeons to test the thickness. 'No, not a hope on that one.'

'You don't think you're going to get out

of here in one piece do you?' chuckled one of the rats. 'You'll be lucky if you see the light of day tomorrow … ha, ha … When *she's* finished with you you'll know all about the power of the Scarlet Queen,' and the cell fell silent again.

The fairies huddled dejected and despondent in the corner of the miserable, odious fortress. The rats sat back on the floor on the side of the cell door that would not crunch them again should it open with its usual gusto. They proceeded to down the ale they had hidden about their bodies when the Queen had entered in case she confiscated it. The more they drank, the merrier they became and started singing in a bawdy manner.

*'We've got the Rainbow Fairies
and they don't know where they are.
Now they're with the Queen of Outlands …
they will not be going very far!'*

As they got drunker and drunker, they slumped lower and lower until the large ring of gaoler keys attached to fat rat's belt dangled onto the floor. After a while Iris stood up and challenged them, 'I bet you can't drink all of that in one mouthful.' The other fairies muffled a smile and a snigger when they realised what Iris was doing.

'What do you mean, you stupid fairy, you've got no idea how much we can drink,' one of the rats retaliated in a slurred, almost incoherent tone.

'Oh go on, show us,' championed Fern.

'How disgusting,' squealed Buttercup in a tone of excitement.

Mouthful followed mouthful as the rats guzzled down the ale. Gulp, gulp, gulp was followed by snores and snorts, which rumbled through the cell as the rats gradually slumbered into a state of total oblivion.

Iris leapt to her feet, turned round to the fairies and hushed them, then crept up to one of the rats and detached the keyring from his belt. Because it was so heavy, Iris dropped it to the floor with an enormous clatter. The whole cell fell silent as the rats stopped snoring, and the fairies braced themselves and shrank back against the wall in terror. It seemed like an eternity before the rats started spluttering again and fell back to sleep. The fairies heaved a huge sigh of relief and slid to the ground.

'Quick,' urged Iris and they ran back to the rats and grabbed the keys.

'How are we going to reach the lock?' exclaimed Petal. Then of course they all looked at the height of the door handle and lock looming above them.

'On each other's shoulders,' urged Poppy.

So up they all popped onto each other's shoulders until Iris fluttered to the top dragging the enormous keyring upwards. Once on top, Iris manhandled one of the huge keys into the lock, but it was not the right one.

'Hurry up,' loudly whispered Poppy who was at the bottom of the fairy chain. 'You're all a bit heavy.'

'I'm going as quick as I can,' came the exasperated reply from Iris. 'I just have to find the right key.' As time marched on, the tension grew and the fairies were fearful of being caught. Iris tried another, but it was the third and final one she tried that opened the door. The fairies repeated the exercise from the outside to lock the rats in.

Once in the corridor the air was much warmer than in the cell. All along the walls of the corridors hung gargoyles carved out of wood. However, as the fairies looked closer they noticed that they had faces with eyes that were following every movement the fairies made. A faint breath was coming out of their noses (which they could touch with their tongues), but other than that, they were mute and had no bodies.

'I wish I could do that,' cried Poppy as

she attempted to get her tongue to reach her nose.

'They are alive!' exclaimed Fern as she stared at them. They responded by giving a sad, helpless expression.

'Come on Fern, there's nothing we can do,' nudged Iris as they stood pondering. The whole place was pitch black.

'Which way now?' enquired Bluebell.

'I don't know,' Iris said shrugging her shoulders.

As they stood for a while, shuddering, whilst deciding on their next move, a soft cold whoosh spun around encircling them and whisking them about. At first it was faint and dark, but as it gained momentum the current got greyer and greyer and faster and faster, then it hooped up like a vortex in front of them. Ahead stood a white apparition, a male form with long, straight grey hair, and a long, straight grey beard triangularly pointed to his toes. It was difficult for the fairies to judge whether he was a man or not. He looked similar but he had ears which were larger than normal and were elongated at both ends. He wore a white gown down to his bare feet, held a shepherd's crook in his right hand and a large ornate crucifix encrusted with sparkling stones and jewels rested on his chest.

'I am Gabriel, Father of all Angels,' he said. 'I am pleased to meet you. Where are the Angel Children?'

'What Angel Children?' asked Fern.

'The Angel Children who are going to help us,' he replied.

'Help you do what?' questioned Buttercup, starting to look very puzzled whilst the rest of the fairies began fidgeting in an uncomfortable fashion.

'Get back my power of course, and then I shall be able to take back my Kingdom from the Scarlet Queen. She defeated me in the Battle between Good and Evil, stole my land, burned our crucifixes and turned my subjects into wooden gargoyles, hanging them on these walls as you see. She gloats over them as trophies. She can be as hot as the devil from hell and can burn or make wood of anything she wants by pointing that ruby waist clasp at them. *That* clasp is mine and used to be the brightest, clearest, purest diamond in the whole of my Kingdom. She seized it from me, turned it into a ruby and made it hers. That is how she took my power and uses it in all its extremes,' said Gabriel, shaking his staff in the air and banging it down on the ground next to them in anger.

The fairies recoiled at the thud, scrunching into each other in a huddle with fear at the outburst.

Calmly, Gabriel then continued, 'You have to help the Angel Children when they come to Outlands tonight, or else ...' he tailed off momentarily, then continued '... or else there will be no more Christmases

. . . ever again, for ever, and all the good in the world will be undone and never exist any more.'

The fairies all gasped together and held their breath for what seemed like an eternity. When they had taken the information in, they all slowly exhaled in disbelief (they tended to do most things in unison).

'Well my . . .' Petal finally exclaimed. 'That's a tall order.' She frowned, quite forgetting the gravity of the situation and that they were in the company of a very important person.

'Yes indeed,' replied Gabriel, 'a very tall order indeed,' which was then echoed by the voices of the other fairies. 'Mmmm . . . a very tall order . . .'

Gabriel snapped his fingers and their temporary distraction instantly disappeared as the fairies jumped to attention like soldiers (the only thing that wasn't quite right was that they were not in uniforms, rather more colourful dresses).

However, Gabriel now had their complete attention.

'How exactly do you think we are going to find the Angel Children here, let alone risk their lives in such a dangerous place with such an evil woman?' asked Poppy.

'Trust me, they will find you and you *must* assist them. My dears, they are already aware of the consequences if they don't do anything,' replied Gabriel most earnestly. 'Farewell my friends, for now,' and with a flash of white light and puff of smoke, Gabriel had vanished.

'Phew . . .' they all said together and then fell into quiet contemplation as they considered just what to do next.

CHAPTER 5

Santa's Grotto

As the two huge, black leather boots confronted them and an enormous, jolly '*Ho, ho, ho*' echoed through the air, the children slowly raised their eyes as if they were ascending all the way to heaven. They saw red trousers tucked into the black boots and these were trimmed with brilliant white fur. A huge circumference of black belt hid the rest of the body. Then the children craned their heads backwards until they could see the entire scene. The top half of the body was clearly a man with white tousled hair protruding from beneath a conical, floppy red cap also trimmed with brilliant white fur which had a bobble on the end to match. The man's beard was as white as the pure driven snow. He had a broad face, a large round belly and overall he was chubby and plump. He was everything the children had anticipated Santa Claus to be – quite amazing ...

They were dumbstruck until Christian asked, 'Are you a real Santa Claus, or one of those we see in department stores?'

Santa chuckled and his tummy shook when he laughed. 'Yes, I am the "real" Santa and your sister Gemma has already met my helpers – the dwarves and the fairies. However, we have no time for that, you have a most pressing task ahead of you so you must make haste.'

With her usual matter-of-factness Lorna enquired, 'Make haste for what?'

Gemma gasped, but Christian had already seen the excitement of an adventure ahead of them and asked, 'Yes please, what are we going to do?'

'Oh do be quiet, Christian, you really are

quite stupid, you don't know where we are, who this man is and what he is expecting us to do ... and besides ...' Lorna continued in full flow '... we are not in any position whatsoever to stay here, let alone do anything. Come on both of you, we must go back to Uncle Nicholas's house now or else we will be in trouble and ... more to the point,' she breathlessly continued, 'if we don't get back soon, the *real* Santa Claus will know we aren't in bed and won't come and leave us some presents,' Lorna said for the benefit of Gemma's ears.

'Ho, ho, ho' chuckled Santa again. 'I must say you've got a point young lady and it's perfectly true that Santa may well not visit you tonight; however he won't be visiting anybody tonight unless you are able to do something.'

With as much courage as she could muster, Gemma asked, 'If we do help you, we won't have enough time before Christmas Day tomorrow.'

Santa smiled and bowed his head down to Gemma and said, 'Time is a human phenomenon and does not have the same meaning here – it is always Christmas in here. *She* has ruled that there will never be a Christmas again by invoking the *Royal Puritan Decree, the Queen's Command.*'

'Who is "*she*"?' enquired Christian with eager anticipation.

'*She*,' replied Santa, 'is the Scarlet Queen and is an evil-doer. She doesn't want anyone to have a Christmas, nor have fun or happiness. She has stolen the power and the right from Gabriel, Father of all Angels, to rule his Kingdom, the Kingdom of Outlands, and she calls it her "Queendom". He is a good man and she is a wicked woman. There are no seasons any more, it is dark all the time and she relies on what the spirits are telling her. With her she always has three ugly wizened witches. They help her contact the spirits and she does what the spirits say. However as long as the Scarlet Queen possesses the ruby waist clasp, she will always have ultimate control.'

The children gasped with horror at the words of Santa. Stuttering now, Christian asked, 'Wh-where does she live?'

Santa replied, 'She lives in a turreted palace, called Volcanus, way out to the north of here, perched high on the top of a hollow mountain and surrounded by dark hills and black streams. But before you get to that, there is the murky marsh and bog land. This is where the biting beetles and munching mosquitoes hang out to protect the Queen from intruders.

'Once you step outside our Grotto you enter a whole different world of fear, poverty and deprivation. There are no happy, smiling children playing with their toys and no joyous families enjoying each others' company. She has invoked her *Royal Puritan Decree*, *The Queen's Command* which means no recreation, no gifts and . . . no Christmas!'

The children were aghast and horrified at the thought.

Santa continued, 'She has kidnapped the fairies so that she can stop me taking presents to the children of Outlands. The fairies and the dwarves help me make and deliver them and she knows that I cannot do that without them. But, more importantly, she wants to get you into Volcanus.'

'Why does she want us in the palace?' asked a bemused Christian.

'The runes are telling the Queen that there may be a challenge to her power and she is getting very nervous. Talk is that she has had the names of children spelt out in the runes ...' he halted momentarily and then continued '... your names, the names of the Angel Children. You must now overthrow the Scarlet Queen.'

Fear ran over the faces of the children. Gemma went positively pale, Christian looked very strange and Lorna extremely concerned.

'No, no, absolutely not,' commenced Lorna. 'It's quite out of the question. We are simply not able to do anything against the might of this woman ... and after all, she's much more powerful than us.'

'Now, now children, you've heard the story of "David and Goliath" haven't you? It's not a case of physical strength, it's about wit and guile and using your talents to overcome the powers of oppression and wrong doing.'

'Phew,' sighed Gemma, 'that's a tall order. Oh, I'm really not sure that we would be of any use.'

'Definitely, no use, no use whatsoever,' repeated Lorna, trying to convince the others.

'Well, I have to say I think it's a brilliant idea. How exciting, when can we go?' asked Christian.

'Oh no Christian, we are *not* going,' replied Lorna.

Santa, the children and the entire

workshop fell quiet as they all thought very long and hard about the situation.

From the corner of the workshop, Morsel appeared. 'Psst!' broke the silence. 'Psst, over here.' He beckoned the children with his index finger. 'Follow me.' He led them over to a solid cathedral-styled oak door, ran up it and bounced upon the latch. The door sprang open revealing the outside world beyond. Haggis led the way out and the children followed. As the children peered around, the air was grey and foggy, the trees were sad and droopy and everything was coloured brown – brown houses, brown gardens, brown animals and ... very miserable people.

'I must show you what we mean,' said Haggis, leading them to a very small, very shabby hut, barely thatched and full of gaps in the walls. In trepidation, the children looked behind them to take comfort from the sight of the door they had come

through, but there was no door to be seen –
just the image of a faded, sad-looking
Christmas tree with its brown needles pointing to the ground like long, lanky fingers.

They approached the hut and Haggis
gently tapped on one of the shutters. The
shutter slowly opened and a strained eye
protruded from the faint light within. 'It's
me, Haggis,' whispered Haggis to the
occupant.

'Oh, Haggis, it's you,' came a whispered
reply from within. 'I'll let you in, but you
must hurry and be very quiet.'

The children stooped through the tiny
frame and followed Haggis into the hut. It
was a very small room, with not much in the
way of furniture and the occupants were
pixies. (Gemma had also seen what pixies
looked like from a book and so was able to
recognise them.) They were very petite
pixies and were all wearing very dowdy
brown clothes. The children were smart
enough to realise that their own lives were

far removed from the lives of the hut dwellers. The male pixie introduced himself as Art, his wife as Esther and his two children as Erin and Aron. The little hut dwellers had been sitting round a miniature gnarled wooden table sharing a paltry meal of bread and broth. They all looked very sad and the children were very upset and moved when they saw the sight before them. This was because of the paleness and poverty which they saw in Art's hut.

'Angel Children,' applauded Art as he softly clapped his hands together and then fell to his knees in front of them. 'We have been waiting for you so long. You are our saviours, but we cannot wait any longer and must make now make haste. Esther has packed a small amount of provisions for our journey,' he announced as he launched a compact knapsack onto his back and set off towards the door. It was touching that whatever small provisions they had, they were willing to share with the children.

'Where are we going?' asked Christian before Art had opened the door.

'Shush,' hushed Art. 'The walls have eyes, the roof has ears and the earth remembers everything.'

Gemma, thinking this was a rather peculiar comment asked, 'Do you mean we are not alone?'

'Certainly not alone, my child, we can but sneeze and the Scarlet Queen will know. But you should be all right as you have human blood which is cold and does not give out a scent,' replied Art.

'Getting back to the journey,' intercepted Lorna in her usual factual tone, 'you didn't say where are we going.'

'Ah, yes of course, I digress. I am directing you to Volcanus to conquer the Scarlet Queen,' replied Art.

The children gasped . . .

'Oh golly!' shrieked Gemma as quietly as she could.

After the initial shock sank in, Lorna

ventured, 'But how are we supposed to get in there? Santa says the place is a fortress.'

'Trust me,' said Art. 'You are the Angel Children and you can do things you never imagined, nor ever knew you would be able to do. Gabriel will protect you and equip you for the task ahead. He knows you have the ability to do his good and carry out his will . . .' Art's words tailed away and hung in the air above the children.

The children were unable to describe what happened next, but it was as though a prism illuminated their minds and all thoughts of anxiety and concern were washed away in the cascade of colour which lightened their senses. A mixed feeling of euphoria and giddiness lifted their spirits and raised their souls to the sky above and temporarily they were elated. They were now ready to face the challenge which lay ahead.

After that strange experience the children,

who had previously been very worried about the things that were going on and where they would end up, now had a distinctly different viewpoint and had got themselves quite fully into the adventure. All the fear and apprehension had disappeared and a willingness filled their hearts and minds when they realised what they could do and how important they were. With renewed vigour (and just a little bit of nervous anticipation) they marched out after Art. Christian (as probably expected by all) led the way with Lorna at the back and Gemma sandwiched in the middle (for safety).

The world outside the hut was eerie and bleak. The scenery was brown and dowdy and there was no other movement around them. Art led the way followed very closely by the children as they went deeper into the dark, dank woodland which was Art's home. They crunched over woodland debris, splitting twigs underfoot. Art urged them to be as quiet as possible, but it was difficult as the light was so faint. In the distance they could make out the sound of trickling water and as they got nearer and nearer the sound got louder and louder, until they came to the reason for the noise. It was hard to make out what the shape was, but what they could quite definitely see was the colour of the water. To their horror, the waterfall ran black and cascaded in torrents of black froth at their feet. It lapped and licked around their toes, almost drawing them into it. As they jumped back when the tide rushed towards them, they heard a noise like a horn, hollow and flat, a long and low crescendo at the crest of the waterfall. It was uncanny and frightening and numbed the atmosphere.

The children looked up to see the silhouette of a magnificent, majestic white winged unicorn on the skyline staring up toward heaven. His entire shape glowed in the darkness, his spiral gold horn shone and his dark eye sparkled.

'That's Nadir, ruler of the empire of Zenith, of which Outlands is part. He has returned to reinstate his Kingdom with the impending recapture of Outlands. He has come to watch you on your way. We must make haste,' confirmed Art. With that, Nadir faded from view.

CHAPTER 6

Volcanus

The fairies stood for a while in silence in the miserable corridor.

'Which way now?' enquired Buttercup.

'I don't know,' replied Iris.

'What about this way?' suggested Bluebell, pointing in one direction. It looked exactly the same as the other direction.

'No, I don't think so,' responded Fern.

'Well, we have to do something,' voiced Poppy.

'Absolutely,' responded Petal. 'Just what, though?'

'Come on,' insisted Bluebell. 'We have to

go one way or the other.' So off they marched ... two one way and four the other! When they realised what they had done, the two spun round and ran to join the other four.

'We must stick together,' yelled Poppy.

'I know, I know, don't shout at me,' retaliated Fern and hitched her emerald dress from round her ankles. Their pace quickened with what dim light there was provided by the twinkling eyes of the petrified gargoyles, who seemed to be willing them on their way. The appearance of the corridor changed little as they cautiously wended their way across the cold flags. A faint hum began to permeate the air and as they approached, the louder it became. The fairies hesitated and all but stopped in their tracks as the hum turned into a chant and the chant turned into a monotonous wail.

'As we mix we stir the pot
The slugs and snails so ripe and hot,
We crunch, we cream into a lotion
And put the potion into motion ...'

Silently they crept towards the source of the sound, none of them wishing to be heard or seen as they bunched up outside the cavernous door. The chanting halted and the fairies held their breath as they waited. It started again ...

'Eye of Iris, Foot of Fern
Boil up Bluebell and Buttercup burn,
Pummel Poppy and Petal squash
The thought of Christmas we will quash...'

The three wicked witches cackled and laughed as they leapt and sprang round the bubbling cauldron. They looked like most people imagine witches to be – ugly, old, ashen faces, manic sunken eyes, long, protruding, warted noses and their shapeless bodies clad in manky black, dowdy smocks. They of course had the customary pointy hats which flopped over with age and covered their lanky, grey rat's-tail hair.

'What is that I smell, Giselle?' asked Esmerelda.

'Mmmm ... Methinks our ingredients may have arrived,' Esmerelda chuckled.

'Tut, tut, tut,' smiled Pandora and rubbed her hands together with glee.

The three witches crept to the door and heaved it open, and the fairies, who had been listening on the other side, fell through on top of each other.

'How wonderful,' enthused Esmerelda. 'So, so perfect.'

'They can go straight into the cauldron now and ferment nicely for hours!' shrieked Giselle.

'Oh absolutely ... so, so absolutely,' agreed Esmerelda.

'Perhaps not so quick. We ought to have

a little fun with these specimens, don't you think, girls?' taunted Pandora.

'Let's hang them from the spider's web above and they can mature,' suggested Giselle.

'What an excellent idea, quite excellent,' enthused Pandora. 'Where did you put the peg bats?'

'Over in the beetle box,' replied Giselle.

'Are the beetles out today?' enquired Esmerelda.

'Some are, some aren't, some are sharpening their teeth in anticipation of the children's arrival,' confirmed Giselle.

'Should be really exciting,' cackled Pandora, 'I so love barbaric entertainment,' spitting out the tail of a newt, the rest of which she had been chewing. 'They're so bitter, those lime-green things, I wonder if that fairy in the green frock will taste any better . . .?'

The fairies shrank back into the shadows and cowered against the nearest wall, from

64

which was hanging an amazing array of bones, fur and skins.

'Yuk!' shrieked Fern as she leant her neck against the entrails of a goblin.

'Look at the state of my dress,' cried Iris as she brushed down the skirt. 'This really is totally, totally unacceptable and quite demeaning to say the least, just you wait until the Angel Children arrive, then you'll be sorry,' wagging her finger at the witches.

'I don't think you've grasped the enormity of the situation, Iris,' added Petal as she stood shuddering in the corner. 'I think we are just about to become a rather drawn-out meal for them.'

Now as the fairies waited to see their fate, the witches had got the peg bats out of the beetle box. A few inquisitive beetles popped their heads out of the void to have a look around, but they soon resumed their sharpening with renewed vigour at the prospect of biting the children. The peg bats were actually squashed-faced bats with protruding, bulbous white eyes, who swooped up and down and round and round. They grabbed each fairy by their shoulders, plucked them off the ground and swung them onto the threads of the enormous, matted cobweb hanging from the roof of the cavern. The sudden jerking movement of the dangling process alerted the black widow spider from her dreamy slumbers and she ventured forth to investigate.

'Ah ha, me lovelies, what have we here? ... Me finks I do see a veritable feast, me finks ... yum, yum. Me finks they be very tasty ...' prodding Poppy in her rather podgy stomach.

'Get away from me you revolting vampire.'

'Ah a feisty one, me finks – all the more pleasure in the digestion,' – licking her lips with a salacious grin – 'me do likes a little fight when sampling the rare delights of sweeter grub than goblins ... yes, yes, yum, yum.'

A shout came from below. 'Just you keep your grubby mitts off them, Spits, they're ours, we got them first and they're just hanging around until we're ready to put them in the pot.'

'Hisssss ...' Spits spat out and ejected a load of sticky froth as she reluctantly recoiled back into the abyss of her solitary world, muttering nasty things about the witches under her breath. She was very grumpy and put out by the fact that she had a perfectly adequate take-away meal on her plate and couldn't make the most of it.

The witches busied themselves with further preparation of the brew:

'Toe of frog, slime from the bog,
eye of fish, flavours the dish.
Sting of nettle, finger of Petal,
thorn of bramble, wax from the candle.'

And so on ...

Frankly the fairies were now pretty fed

up but there wasn't a lot they could do, save flapping their arms and legs around and to cap it all, their dresses were well and truly beyond ruined. From a bird's-eye view the fairies could see the three witches' broomsticks lined up beside the fireplace, and as the witches' chants reached a crescendo and the flames leapt higher and even higher, the brooms flew up into the air, circled around the fairies and fell to the ground with an almighty crack. The cauldron bubbled and then the cavern fell weirdly silent.

CHAPTER 7

The Whirlwind

After the appearance of Nadir, Art and the children trudged on past the Black Lake and into Tall Tree Forest. The tree barks were the tallest the children had ever seen, forming a crown of leaves at the very top, creating an enshrouding canopy under which they walked. They often tripped and stumbled on the forest debris. Gemma was the first to fall, grazing her knee on the carpet of pine needles upon which she landed. A trickle of blood ran down her leg onto the ground and a droplet of tear trickled down her cheek. But she bravely soldiered on. The air began to chill around them and of course they had left Uncle Nicholas's house in such a hurry that they were all still wearing their nightclothes, dressing gowns and slippers, not very suitable attire for the sort of journey they had embarked upon. Gemma had tucked the feather neatly into her dressing gown pocket. A stirring in the high leaves signalled the presence of an owl who settled on a branch close to them and hooted them on their way. He hopped from branch to branch at their sides as if marshalling them through the precarious Tall Tree Forest with some form of safety. Specks of rain drizzled through the pine needles, pattering on and off the foliage and making the visibility even more difficult.

Lorna, who was not really a physically active person, struggled with the exertion and for once wished she could be tucked up in her warm bed back at the vicarage. She also wondered what they were going to find and what they were going to do when they got there. Due to the drudgery of the hike, even for Christian the enthusiasm and excitement of the adventure had started to dwindle slightly.

They reached a clearing in the forest where a little light penetrated, but the sky above them was still grey and misty. Art suggested they rested for a time and they sat down on a circle of stones surrounding what appeared to be a rocky plateau, which could almost have been a table as the whole arrangement resembled a dining setting. As the children sat, Art shared out what few provisions he had brought and whilst they were only simple cheese sandwiches and blackcurrant juice, the children were grateful. For a while they became very drowsy and closed their eyes with tiredness whilst Art kept watch.

The children were woken with a shudder as Art shook their shoulders to stir them. As they opened their eyes, they knew a change had taken place. They looked down at their clothing, which was now no longer night attire but had been replaced with something completely different and not something they would have chosen in a shop back home. They were now wearing warm, hessian smocks over fawn calico shirts and trousers down to substantial leather sandals. Holding their smocks in place were wide belts, and over their backs both Lorna and Gemma carried a small cane bow with a sheath containing three wooden arrows and Christian possessed a sword and shield. To their surprise, around their necks hung gold crucifixes on coarse metal chains with quite large rings. The transformation was complete, the expedition had commenced.

A million questions ran through their minds as they gazed in amazement at their new outfits. They looked every inch warriors and gazed imploringly at Art, seeking answers. Art read their minds, but just put his fingers to his lips implying that they should hush.

Art whispered, 'We must make haste, the Scarlet Queen will know that you are now on the way. Her warthogs will soon be on my scent, if they are not already. She would rather capture you and take control rather than let you get into Volcanus yourself and find the fairies.'

A grunt rang out in the distance, then another and another. The children froze and Art stiffened. 'The warthogs are on the way, they are behind us. They will have picked up any sign of where we have walked. Quick, quick, we must hide,' hurried Art. It was then Gemma realised that the speck of blood on the Tall Tree Forest floor which had bled from her knee had led them nearer.

The grunts got closer and closer and louder and louder until it felt like the warthogs were coming towards them from all directions. Art found a tree hollow and ushered them in, and as they huddled together crouched on the sandy floor an enormous whirlwind whistled up outside the bark. Within an instant the entrance to the hollow had been completely sealed with leaves and branches and the occupants were shrouded in darkness. Terrified, they listened as the grunts drew so close they could almost feel the clammy sweat of the warthogs beyond the barrier. Not a flinch of their bodies gave their location away as they waited for what seemed like an age, when it was really only minutes. They scarcely breathed in fear. After a while, the grunts subsided only to be replaced by spine-chilling squeals of painful agony piercing the night air.

No-one dared to speak and they remained motionless in their hideaway. Eventually Art quietly ventured, 'I think they've gone now but we must be careful, they could be hiding nearby ready to spring upon us as we appear again.' They continued to wait, unable to speak until the obstruction between them and the warthogs started to fall away. As they watched in horror, the leaves and branches were gradually being brushed away by sweeping tentacles from up high, and daylight once again rushed into their imposed tomb. Slowly and cautiously they crept to the opening and looked out. The tree's branches had cleared their exit and the forest debris which had been their captor had been piled high. Terror was written across the faces of the children as they saw the scene before them. The warthogs lay on top of the leaves and branches and thick, acrid smoke rose away from their funeral pyre.

As they walked away their pallid complexions showed the seriousness of their situation. They trooped without speaking a word in single file behind Art as he led them out of Tall Tree Forest.

'And this, my friends, is where I leave

you. The rest of this journey is now down to you. Take heart that those who try, succeed, and those who succeed are welcomed into the Kingdom of Heaven. Show courage and determination and you will reap the rewards you so desire. Your path now lies directly ahead. Follow the glow of the North Star and it will lead you to your destination.'

With these words, each child in turn thanked and hugged him and Art turned and bade them farewell.

CHAPTER 8

Nadir, King Of Zenith

They waited a while and gathered their thoughts together. Lorna was the first to speak. 'Well, there's no turning back now,' she said, much as though she probably wished they could. Christian's enthusiasm had also lessened somewhat, but he wasn't going to let the girls see that as he felt he was now in charge and the responsibility gave him quite a positive boost. Gemma was certainly bewildered, wishing perhaps that she had never stumbled across Morsel in the hallway at the vicarage.

'Come on,' rallied Christian. 'Standing around here isn't going to get us very far,' and off they marched once again. Their journey over the plains proved to be uneventful as they followed the glow of the North Star, until the ground beneath their feet got damp and sticky and walking grew harder and harder. It became an arduous trudge, and they were barely able to lift one foot in front of the other. At the same time, the sky was filled with black clouds ahead of them.

'Ouch!' squealed Gemma and she smacked her hand against her bare wrist. As she looked down she realised she had splatted a mosquito dead onto the palm of her hand. 'Yuk!' she cried as she picked off the bloodied mosquito and dropped it. She looked at Christian and Lorna who had mosquitoes in their hair. 'You've got them in your hair!' she shrieked and putting her hand to her head, realised they were crawling all over her, too. She looked down and saw that shiny black beetles were biting her toes. They all three jumped and ran around screaming, flailing their arms and slapping their bodies like monkeys and making a terrible noise.

Their frantic racket was silenced by the doleful horn crescendo. They looked up and in their midst stood the towering frame of Nadir. It was a frightening sight. The beetles stopped biting and the mosquitoes stopped munching and fell away, retreating to their slimy sanctuary. Nadir bent down on his front knees.

'I think he wants us to get on his back,' said Christian.

'I can't do that,' cried Lorna.

Nadir waited patiently and in silence.

'Oh come on,' yelled Christian, 'don't be such a sissy!' as he hoisted himself up onto the animal's broad withers. He pulled Gemma up behind him and Lorna took position at the back. The unicorn regained his composure and shot forth up into the sky above, in full flight across the bog. The chill wind flew past their faces and their hair and smocks blew with the movement. Christian couldn't work out what speed they were doing, but the elation and adrenalin rush was so stimulating, it stirred excitement within them. The unicorn's wingspan pounded the air around them. They seemed to be airborne for ages, passing over dark hills and black streams, all the time heading towards the bright glistening of the North Star.

As they began their descent, their ears popped a little and they swallowed hard to relieve the pressure. In the distance, a grey speck on the horizon turned out to be a turreted palace. They were near Volcanus. The unicorn slowed to the ground not far from the palace and came gently to a halt. No words were necessary, save 'Thank you,' and as the children realised that the rest of the task lay in their hands, their blood ran cold through their veins. As with Art, Nadir was gone in an instant. The children checked their bows and arrows were still in place and tidied their clothes.

Christian, as the only male, felt it was his duty to take the lead. He took a very deep breath and said, 'This is it, the final stage, we must be brave and stay together.' Neither of the girls said anything, they just nodded their heads in acknowledgement. Lorna coughed quietly to clear her throat (even though she didn't need to, it was just a reaction to her fear) and stepped forward. The three trooped in single file towards the palace. It was a very tall, thin, square-shaped building with even taller cylindrical turrets to each corner. At the top of each turret a black flag flew, which was emblazoned with a scarlet cross with the face of a wicked-looking woman above it. The children knew that this would be what the Scarlet Queen looked like. Courage and determination drove them forward as the mausoleum towered above them. The narrow slitted windows were protected with iron bars and the drawbridge was up, massive chains holding it firmly closed. Huge red, roaring fires flamed from the pinnacle of the four crown-shaped turrets and numerous bonfires surrounded the palace perimeter, glowing amber and scarlet against the blackness. The sight was overwhelming and the children could feel the heat from the furnaces way back where they were standing.

Gemma asked the obvious question. 'How are we going to get in, then?'

'I don't know!' snapped Christian. 'Well, we did expect it to be a fortress, didn't we?'

'Well I have to ask, just what did you expect the nastiest woman in Outlands to live in? An unguarded, flimsy tent and invite in any passing strangers?' added Lorna.

'I don't know, it's not my fault,' replied Christian.

'Mmm,' mused Gemma, 'bit of a tricky one.'

'Tricky one, to say the least,' agreed Lorna.

'Don't suppose there's a door bell?' Gemma asked.

Christian burst into peals of laughter. 'Door bell? . . . door bell?' he repeated until his sides ached, then blurted out, 'Oh yes, of course, what a good idea. Let's ring it and see if Jeeves the friendly butler welcomes us in for tea with the Queen. Get real, Gem, we might be welcomed in, because *we will* be tea for the Queen!'

'You don't need to be so sharp with me, brainbox. Let's hear your great idea then?' Gemma turned her face away and was clearly upset by Christian's harsh words. Lorna read her reaction and momentarily sympathized. 'Was a bit of a dumb idea, Gem. We have to get in there unseen, find the fairies, overthrow the Queen and all get out alive . . . again unseen.'

'Seems such a simple plan, doesn't it?' grimaced Gemma. 'Just a teeny bit harder in reality . . .'

None of the children had any bright ideas as they thought about the enormity of the situation. After her last suggestion, Gemma was reluctant to put forward any more ideas for fear of being shot down in flames again.

'Don't suppose there's a back door where the tradesmen go in?' offered Lorna.

Equally now Lorna got the amused rebuke from Christian. 'Oh yes, topping, absolutely topping. We'll hide behind the back of the milk float as the milkman takes in his early morning deliveries ... I don't suppose she even knows what a cow is, let alone have cereal!'

'Christian, I really think that you are now being very unhelpful, so stop having a go at us. I've not heard *you* saying anything useful, in fact nothing of any note at all,' stuttered Lorna.

With that comment, Christian backed down and became quite thoughtful. 'You know you could just be right in some way,' he remarked. 'There must be another way of getting in which the cleaners use or something.'

'I somehow doubt she has cleaners, but somebody or something ...?' Lorna tailed off.

'Perhaps a cook like Betty?' Then after a few thoughtful seconds '... erm ... well perhaps not!' added Gemma.

Christian had started to walk round in circles (like older folk do when they are mulling things over) and also putting his hand to his chin for the same reason (like an older man would). It must have worked because he came up with a very good idea. 'I think we ought to go and look around the outside of the palace to see if there is a back door or something,' he said.

In the absence of any other reasonable suggestion they had to agree and set forth to circumnavigate the palace walls. As with all palaces in stories (and this one is no exception), it was surrounded by a moat, but the difference was that this moat was filled with black water which bubbled like a kettle of boiling water. Cautiously the children drew nearer. Curiously something red and slimy jumped out of the water and plopped back in.

'What on earth was *that*?' exclaimed Christian, leaping back in astonishment and falling back into the two girls who had been peering from behind him.

'There it is again,' shrieked Gemma, pointing at another one which made a huge splash in front of them and soaked their clothing with black gunk.

'Another one, look over there!' exclaimed Lorna.

'And there, and there,' added Christian. Actually they were now popping up and down all over the moat so that the children could see quite clearly that they were a type of fish, but not like the ones we have in our ponds and seas. Some of them had two huge heads at one end, others had huge heads at both ends and they were decidedly ugly with gargantuan mouths, cream fangy exposed teeth and completely white starey eyes. One of the fish leapt out of the water, lurched towards Christian and bit him on the finger.

'Ouch, you nasty thing,' squealed Christian as he managed to bat it to the moat with its other hand. It also squealed as it fell back and into the black water. The fish were now quite frantic and seemed to be highly disturbed by the presence of the children; in fact the feeling was quite mutual so the children hurried away, retreating from the edge of the abyss. Christian looked at his hand and saw that the fish's fangs had made quite a deep cut which was now starting to weep. He knew that he shouldn't put it into his mouth because of the risk of infection so he grabbed part of his calico tunic and wrapped his finger in it and soldiered on. They followed a narrow path which had appeared through some tall bulrushes, but they found it hard to see very far ahead as they were much smaller in comparison. Christian led the way and the others followed almost on tiptoes.

All of a sudden, Christian stopped abruptly. The bulrushes had given way to a clearing and Christian had now got a better view. 'Shush.' He put his fingers to his lips as he turned to Gemma and Lorna. 'Look over there,' he said, pointing in the direction of the palace with his other hand. On a track some distance in front of them was an old-fashioned horse and cart and sitting in the driving seat was an old-fashioned goblin puffing at a pipe. However, what was not old-fashioned but very bizarre was that the horse was pushing the cart and occupant backwards. The whole thing was going backwards with seemingly no apparent problem and appeared, as far as they were concerned, quite normal.

'How strange, how very strange,'

remarked Christian yet again putting his hand to his chin in the mature, thoughtful way that he had now developed.

'Forget that for a moment, what's more important is where is he going?' asked Lorna.

'Cripes, that's a point!' cried Gemma. 'Let's watch.'

As they did, they could see that he was heading towards the palace.

'It's going into Volcanus!' exclaimed Christian.

'What's in the cart?' asked Lorna.

'Looks like logs,' replied Christian, 'although it's not easy to tell from here.' They stood as if frozen until Christian said, 'That's it, that's the answer. We stow away in the logs on the back of the cart.'

'You must be joking, he's bound to see us,' said Lorna.

'No, not if we creep up quietly and slip in between the logs, then we'll get into Volcanus unnoticed,' announced Christian.

'Good grief,' gasped Lorna, 'and just how are we going to do that then, clever clogs?'

'Don't know, haven't worked that one out yet,' replied Christian.

'Well, you'd better get your skates on,' intercepted Gemma, 'as he's getting closer to the palace now.'

'Quick, we'll just have to run up and jump onto the back as he's facing the other way,' answered Christian.

Off they scurried, keeping their heads down, trying not to be seen. Thankfully the horse and cart were making slow progress (well it's not that easy walking backwards). They crept round the back and one by one pulled themselves onto the back of the cart. Once on the cart, they tucked themselves under some tarpaulin which had been scrunched up at the rear and waited. The cart bumped over stones on the road and jiggled them around. All three of them held their breath for fear of being spotted by the driver. It seemed like a very long time until eventually the cart drew to a halt. They trembled as they listened to what seemed like a conversation, but they were not words they understood. It was some type of local dialect between the man on the cart and a female voice. The conversation culminated in the clanking of chains and the squeaking of rusty ratchets and then a wooden clang of the drawbridge falling over the moat. The children winced as the sounds vibrated around them.

A jolt shook them and they were off again, rolling over the hollow slatted bridge and on into the austere fortress. Once again, the cart stopped and the occupants waited. Christian took courage and peered out from under the tarpaulin. They were in a courtyard with sand on the floor and high, grey walls all around, and an absolutely putrid smell.

'Phew, what a pong!' Christian recoiled back under cover. 'We're in Volcanus now, we must get out of here in case they start unloading soon.'

They slid off the back of the cart, unfortunately straight on to the floor in front of the driver of the old-fashioned cart and someone else.

CHAPTER 9

Mr Kindling and Mrs Twash

'Yikes!' cried Christian as they stared upwards. In front of them were the cart driver and a very fat goblin woman who was wearing what looked like a maid's outfit.

'Just what 'a' we got 'ere, Mr Kindling?' she asked. (They basically spoke in a very rural dialect but was understandable to the children.)

'Dunno Mrs Twash, but what 'ere they is, they isn't like us,' replied Mr Kindling.

'Please don't hurt us, Mister,' cried Gemma.

'If ida wanted to 'urt yer, I'd 'a' dun it

when yer got in mi cart earlier,' replied Mr Kindling.

'You mean you knew we were in the back of your cart?' asked Lorna.

'Yep, course I did. We might all walk backwards, but we ain't backwards in our 'eads as well,' continued Mr Kindling, pointing to the location of his brain at his temple.

'Actually,' braved Gemma, 'why do you walk backwards?'

'That be the doin' of that nasty Scarlet Queen. When she took over, 'er and 'er wicked witches concocted a spell and cursed us all with walking backwards so we could never run away from 'er kingdom.'

'Gosh, how positively rotten!' cried Gemma.

'Yes, so horrid,' confirmed Lorna.

'Well there ain't nought we can do 'bout it as long as she's 'bout.' Mr Kindling paused. 'So what bring you 'ere then?'

Christian swallowed hard and in his best

voice said, 'We've come to rescue the Rainbow Fairies who the Scarlet Queen has kidnapped from Santa Claus, overthrow her because she has decided to ban Christmas and get out of here alive.' He blurted this out with alarming speed just in case he forgot all the detail.

'"Overthrow" the Scarlet Queen? My word, that's a tall order fer such small pipple,' replied Mr Kindling, 'but I get your drift.'

'Yu ain't be the Angel Children is you then?' asked Mrs Twash.

Lorna cleared her throat. 'Yes, apparently we are, or at least we seem to have been called that,' she responded, still somewhat surprised that their notoriety preceded them.

'Oh champion, just champion,' clapped Mr Kindling. 'Permit us to introduce ourselves, I'd be Woody Kindling an' she'd be Flora Twash, but you ken just call us Woody an' Flora.'

'Pleased to meet you, I am sure,' burst out Lorna, smiling and nodding. 'I am Lorna, this is Christian and this is Gemma,' pointing the other two out in turn.

'Pleased to meet you too, but just one tiny question – just how do you propose to free the fairies and overthrow the Queen?'

'Well, to be honest, we don't really actually know at the moment,' intercepted Christian in his most commanding voice. 'We've got this far, we'll come up with someut,' (accidentally slipping into the vernacular!). Lorna tapped Christian on the arm. 'Sorry, I mean "something".'

'Well we'd betta see what we ken do to 'elp you, ant we Flora?'

'Aye, we'd betta 'ad,' replied Flora.

'That would be awfully nice,' thanked Gemma, the politeness of which received a tiny grin from both Woody and Flora.

'We'd betta 'ave a meeting,' announced Woody and he and Flora walked backwards into the laundry. They all followed (although the children walked forwards). All of the clothes hanging on the washing lines around the room were either red or black. 'They're either 'ers or theirs,' said Woody, meaning the Scarlet Queen and the witches. A goblin child, not much younger than Gemma, sat beside an oval metal washing bowl rubbing clothes up and down a washing dolly. The children had read about these sorts of things in old-fashioned books, but they hadn't actually seen one until then. She did not speak and barely looked up, concentrating on her scrubbing.

Woody informed them that the Rainbow Fairies were in the witches' cavern having been recaptured after escaping from the drunken rats guarding the dungeons. For their incompetence, the rats had been sentenced to five years' hard labour in one of the Scarlet Queen's deepest, darkest coal mines which were managed by the winged wolves. Woody thought it unlikely they would ever be seen again.

Woody continued to give them the information they needed. The witches' cavern was located on the way to the Scarlet Queen's Emporium, so that she could be protected from the enemy.

'What will they do with the Rainbow Fairies?' enquired Lorna.

'Aye, they'll either put 'em in the pot, feed 'em to winged wolves or turn 'em to wooden gargoyles and stick 'em on the walls, all depending on how the Queen feels on the day!'

'How positively ghastly,' remarked Gemma.

'How do you know all this?' asked Christian.

'See all 'em there logs in the cart, they are for the witches' fire to heat the cauldron, so I 'ave to teck 'em logs every day for stokin' the fire so they can get up to their mischief,' replied Woody.

'Golly, that must be frightening, do you not feel scared doing that?' asked Gemma.

'No's, 'cos if they don't get their wood, they don't 'ave a fire, an' if they don't 'ave a fire, they don't 'ave a boiling cauldron, and don't do their spells; so they don't trouble me you see.'

'Seems to work pretty well from what I can see,' commented Christian.

'Aye, that be the case,' replied Woody, 'all's OK so long as they's OK. However, the pipple here are not happy, the children's miserable and disappointed, but what's there to do as long as she's got the power? I gives the pipple extra logs when I can, but it ain't always easy to slip 'em out without some busybody tellin' on you – the walls 'as beady eyes,' lamented Woody.

'Oh dear, that's so sad,' empathised Gemma.

'We have to hatch a plan!' cried Lorna, amazed with her own suggestion and the courage to say that (although she didn't have a clue where to start).

'Hear, hear,' replied Christian without

the faintest idea of what they could possibly do. Reading their willing but frankly blank ponderous faces, Woody said, ''Er power can be broken, you know.'

'How?' asked Christian impatiently.

'She wears a ruby waist clasp, an' as long as she 'as that, she will always have control. She stole the ruby clasp from Gabriel, Father of All Angels – your father in fact.'

'Our father is dead,' interrupted Gemma sharply.

'No, no, not your real father, Gabriel is your spiritual father and leader of your faith. Very powerful man in his own right, but she also stole his full right and faithful followers. The faithful is still faithful, but they can't let it show 'cos she'll punish them. She took out and kept the ruby clasp which was set in Gabriel's crucifix and burnt the rest of them all on a funeral pyre. Heaven was angered and sent about a raging storm, forking lightning with the most magnificent electrical charge ever seen in the Kingdom; torrential flooding rain an' deafening bolts of thunder rocking the core of the earth through the centre and hollowing out Volcanus. 'Tis said that the earth will not rest, the seasons not return and the skies not brighten 'til the Scarlet Queen is laid to rest.'

The children tried to visualise such chaos and upheaval. Christian could see the wrath of the skies striped with white jagged, mechanical tentacles. Lorna thought of the clouds bashing together and tipping their loads of water to earth and Gemma the horrific, deafening crashing of cymbals. They shivered with the thought.

'She survived, but 'tis said that revenge will be wreaked, the core of the earth is enraged and boils with fury ...' Woody tailed off.

As they sat on the wooden stools they watched as Woody drew a layout plan of the palace, using a stick in the sawdust on the floor of the laundry room.

'Here's where we are,' he started, 'an' here's where she is,' he continued. 'Now to get to where she is, you 'ave to get to tuther side of the courtyard, 'ere, go past the dungeons, past the witches' cavern, up the spiral staircase an' into the Queen's quarters in that there turret,' he said, pointing towards the opposite angle of the quadrangle in which they were and then tracing a line up the wall to the turret at the top. 'Now, the courtyard is guarded by goblins like us, but they 'ave bin put under a curse to protect the Queen at all costs. Now we goes past the dungeon an' take laundry to the cavern, which is guarded by two other rats. Then, when you get to the Queen's quarters, you'll be faced with the thirteen-foot-long fire-breathing dragon, called Cassius, protecting 'er chambers,' finished Woody.

'Phew ...' Christian exhaled a long-drawn-out breath. 'Doesn't sound too promising, does it?'

'Cripes, no,' agreed Lorna as she looked at the equipment they had brought with them.

'We cun get you cross the courtyard, can't we Flora?' said Woody nodding towards the clean laundry, 'but we can't get you any further 'cos we'd 'ave to leave you outside the cavern as the laundry's sorted there by rats for the Queen and witches. If we leave you there at midnight, the witches won't be in their cavern as they always meet with the Queen every night at that hour to speak to spirits.'

'Oooh, how very scary,' cried Gemma.

'Well, seems like a good start, but how do we get across the courtyard?' enthused Christian.

'Ahhzz, that's the easy bit,' replied Woody, 'we dress you up as witches,' pointing to the roof-mounted drying rack overhead. Hanging from it were a number of black smocks next to a couple of fitted, shaped scarlet dresses. Beyond the rack, branches on a hatstand supported three battered and rather scrunched witches' tapered hats of varying sizes.

'Yes, a good start ...' announced Lorna, trying not to show the worry in her voice.

'Excellent start,' winced Gemma, pulling her face in desperation.

'But what about thereafter?' Lorna questioned.

'We pretend to be witches!' exclaimed Christian with even greater enthusiasm than he had expressed at any time up until the present moment. 'I don't suppose they have any wands in the laundry too by any chance?' he enquired.

At that remark, they all knowingly tutted and Christian felt duty bound to qualify his comment.

'Well it was a thought, after all we should have the costume and the proper equipment too.'

Their silence told Christian that that discussion had been terminated and they moved on to consider the practicalities of the idea.

'I suggest we better 'ave some grub afore we sends you on your way and we can talk about the detail whilst we nosh.'

Flora Twash turned out to be quite a dab hand not only at laundering clothes but also cooking up a very tasty broth. The children daubed it away with soft, warm bread crusts and washed it down with nettle juice. They all chatted away as they ate and supped and for a time quite forgot what they were doing there and the enormity of the mission ahead of them.

They were brought back to reality with a jolt when Woody informed them of the purpose of the Queen's midnight meeting with the witches. Woody's words 'She gets 'er rune board out,' stopped the chatter dead.

'But we've been taught that those things are terribly evil,' informed Lorna with her usual consternation.

'Aye, that be so, but she's an evil woman with no God-fearing bone in 'er body, so she dunna care. She worships the devil and fears only Satan. She does what Satan directs her to do . . .' Woody tailed off.

'Gosh,' murmured Christian, 'I don't see what hope we have of dealing with her.'

'You must remember that good is always better than evil and that will inspire and guide you to conquer,' said Woody with Flora nodding assertively in the background.

'Ey dunna fear, take flight for the fight, God speed you and he will,' emphasized Flora.

The children set about putting on their disguises over their smocks and rippling with laughter they submerged themselves in the moth-holed and threadbare black cassocks. Gemma was positively swamped in hers and even more so when she put the hat on; she completely vanished save the peeping of her two brown eyes, small nose and tiny mouth just protruding from the midst. Both Christian's and Lorna's cloaks fitted them better and they wriggled their frames to get reasonably comfortable in their new apparel. They both made sure that their faces, hands and feet were as shrouded as possible so as not to draw attention to their identities.

'Perfick, absolutely perfick,' cried Woody with only a slight degree of hesitation as he faced Gemma. 'Nobody will stop yu as yu walks around the quadrangle, but yu still must keep in the shadows of our laundry cart so as not to raise any interest. Dunna speak either as yu be 'eard. If we just gets round as quick as possible, keep yu 'eads down and dunna move a muscle until I tell yu. Wens we gets to t'other side, we leave the laundry at witches' door, we turn back without saying a word and yu must make haste.'

'Thank you very much Mr Kindling, and thank you also Mrs Twash, you have been so kind,' said Lorna in one of her very sincerest of tones and off they went.

*

The cart rumbled over the cobblestones to the side of the open quadrangle, down one of the right angular corridors, creaking and grinding as it bumped and jumped on its wooden wheels. The contents of the cart shifted with the movement. The children hid their faces just enough to see, but the air around them was muggy and misty as they huddled up to each other wedged between the corridor walls and the cart. The wooden gargoyles watched them as they passed by and spiders' webs caught their faces. Their trailing cassocks swept the ground of dirt and sawdust.

Like Woody and Flora, all the dwarves around them walked backwards, acknowledging each other as they passed with short, unrecognisable grunts. The children did not look at them for fear of being recognised. The cart ground to a halt and Woody prodded Christian in his back with his finger and then pointed in the onward direction. No words were spoken as Woody nodded his head in acknowledgement of the handover.

Two rats, one tall and one small, were sitting on three-legged wooden stools on either side of the entrance to the witches' cavern. They had nodded off until the cranking of the cart had roused them from their slumber. The children hid in the blackness underneath the cart and as far out of their view as possible as Woody and Flora unloaded the laundry onto the floor beside the door.

The rats lazily lifted themselves from their stools and sauntered towards the laundry to carry it into the cavern. Woody and Flora stood by the cart, shielding the children from the rats' view. When they had moved all of the laundry, the children's hearts began to race knowing that they had to make a move soon. Their dilemma was solved as Woody struck up a conversation with the rats in a strange language (which the rats understood) and started to draw them away from the witches' cavern by pointing at something in the distance and talking as they ambled away. It seemed as though the rats were quite happy to have a break in their tedious routine, and followed contentedly. Woody was mumbling away and Flora beckoned the children out from under the cart and ushered them through the unguarded entrance, closing the door behind them. Woody returned with the rats, still engrossed in discussion. Flora coughed slightly and said to the rats, 'I'z closed yu door fur yu. Come on Mr Kindling, we must be off now.'

'Ay Mrs Twash, we must be off, off we must be,' replied Woody with a wink of the eye to Flora and with that they turned the cart and trundled back again.

As the children stood on the other side of the door, they heard voices in a language they could understand this time. It was indeed similar to their own native tongue, but they did not know from whom it came. Christian was the first to cure his curiosity as he moved away from the door and ventured forward into the room. Above their heads from the black widow's web, hung the colourful dresses of the Rainbow Fairies, together with the fairies in them.

CHAPTER 10

The Witches' Cavern

'Wow!' exclaimed Christian as all three of them stared round the room with their mouths open.

'Oh flippin' heck, the wicked witches are back.' Bluebell turned to Buttercup with considerable disdain.

The children, who had suddenly remembered that they had been told not to say a word, stood silent. When they realised that the room was empty apart from the hanging articles and their captors (the peg bats), they decided they needed to speak to confirm who they were. Lorna was first. 'We're definitely not witches you know.'

She paused. 'You must be the Rainbow Fairies?' she asked in a rhetorical question sort of way.

'Might be, but who I might ask are you then if you're all dressed up as witches and say you aren't actually witches?' enquired Fern with a degree of concern.

Luckily the peg bats were sound asleep and snoring very loudly as they hung upside down, holding the shoulders of the fairies' dresses on the twines of the cobweb.

Christian pulled up the brim of his rickety hat to reveal his features to the fairies and the two girls did the same to show their rosy complexions.

'My, how pretty you are,' said Poppy to Gemma. 'Oh and you are too, my dear,' looking at Lorna, 'just a bit different though.'

'We've come to save you,' announced Lorna. She was still somewhat put out by Poppy's comment but decided to rise above it and treat it with the contempt it deserved (she'd heard grown-ups use that expression and thought it was appropriate just at that moment).

'Well, dressed like that, we thought you'd come to eat us,' quickly remarked Buttercup.

'No, we definitely prefer fish and chips,' smiled Christian.

'By the way, why are you dressed like that?' enquired Petal.

'It's a longish story ...' Just about to launch into the tale of their travels to date, Christian felt a delicate brush against the back of his neck. He put his hand to the place where the sensation was and felt a furry tingle. He took hold of it to draw it in front of his face to see what it was and shrieked, 'Aaagh, it's gross – get off me you horrid ...' and sprang away from it towards where the fairies were hanging. The girls instinctively joined him and stared at the thing.

'Hisssss ...' Spits spat out again and

ejected another load of sticky froth across the floor towards the children.

'I knows that you wasn't witches when you come in, I coulds smell ye. You doesn't smell the same as real witches and I really likes fresh, pale meat ha ha ...' responded Spits as one of her legs scraped up and down the floor in an expectant fashion. 'A veritable feast methinks, yes indeed a very veritable feast.' Waving a leg she announced, 'One for dinner, one for breakfast and one for lunch, my own delicious gourmet platter ...' as she wiped her tongue round and round her lips '... a very, very veritable feast indeed ...'

'If you come anywhere near us, I'll ... I'll ...' Gemma hesitated.

'You'll what ...? You'll what, young lady?' teased Spits as she rested back on her web tauntingly.

'I don't know just at this very minute ... but I am sure I'll think of something, you disgusting dollop,' Gemma continued.

'I have an idea,' announced Christian, calling the two girls into a powwow with him. They engrossed themselves in deep conversation whilst Spits and the fairies watched, puzzled. The meeting broke up and Christian walked towards Spits, took hold of the edge of her web and tugged it. Spits immediately scurried towards the movement as Christian let go and ran to another part of the web. At the same time Lorna, who had positioned herself at another place by the web, tugged it too. Again Spits immediately scurried towards the movement and Lorna ran away. The Rainbow Fairies were pinging up and down everywhere, but thankfully the peg bats remained asleep.

When it was Gemma's turn to do the same, both Lorna and Christian picked up the web in their hands and folded it over the back and round the head of Spits, wrapping her up and sandwiching her in the middle of the convoluted threads. As she squealed in the midst, the children tied off each of the ends of the threads in knots, completely incarcerating Spits, who punched and shook with anger, rocking the web as she writhed from side to side with frustration.

'I'll get you back, mark my words. When I get out of here, I will stretch every sinew in your pale bodies and glue your guts to every corner of the room and I'll . . .'

'Oh do shut up!' shouted Christian. 'Can't you see we've more important things to do than listen your rubbish?' Spits fell silent and shrank back into her mangled home, ejecting yet more slimy froth in temper. The fairies were still hanging from the bottom of the matted mess of cobweb.

'How are we going to get the fairies down?' asked Lorna.

'Hmm, good question,' replied Christian.

'The peg bats are asleep, which will give us time to work that one out,' suggested Gemma.

'Yes that's true, but none of us can

reach them, we're not tall enough,' mused Lorna.

Gemma sat back on an old three-legged stool and as she did so she realised there was something stopping her from sitting comfortably. It was her bow and set of arrows. 'I've got it, the answer – I've got the answer!' she exclaimed, pulling her bow and arrows out from under the witch's cassock. 'We can fire the arrows at them!'

'Hey presto, she certainly does,' confirmed Christian excitedly.

Now the fairies, who had been watching all of the previous events unfold, understandably tensed up and became exceedingly scared.

'You must be joking!' cried Iris.

'Have you ever fired one of those things before?' enquired Buttercup with obvious concern.

'Well actually not,' was the down-to-earth reply from Gemma, 'but we shall have a jolly good try.'

'Yikes, that speak volumes,' shouted Poppy, wincing backwards.

Both Lorna and Gemma had now got their bows and arrows out and had started to figure out how to fire them.

'How do you get them to shoot?' asked Gemma as she fiddled with the bow, trying to decide which way up it went.

'I don't think the way up really matters,' Christian enlightened her, seizing the bow from Gemma as she was annoying him.

'Right, what you have to do,' instructed Christian, 'is to hold the wooden bendy bit with your left hand, put the arrow resting against the twine and pull back with your right hand, take aim and fire.' To demonstrate the technique, Christian let the arrow go. It whistled out of the holder, shot straight up into the air above, narrowly missing the cobweb complete with fairies and captors, ricocheted off the ceiling and spiralled down, lodging itself neatly in the peak of Lorna's cap.

'Oh, well done, that's a great start!' cried Petal with her eyes nearly popping out of their sockets in shock. 'So unimpressive . . .'

Lorna took off her hat and removed the arrow, carefully avoiding spearing herself in the process. 'Gosh, these spears are terribly sharp,' she remarked.

'Great stuff,' mocked Poppy.

'Come on then Gemma, let's have a go,' urged Lorna.

'Oh no, please don't,' chorused the fairies.

'Have a practice shot, Gemma, just like I did,' enthused Christian and he started to repeat his instructions, this time assisting her as she went through the motions. 'Again, hold the wooden bendy bit with your left hand, put the arrow resting against the twine. No, no, put the spear end next to the wooden bendy bit, not the other way round or else it will go backwards.' Christian was getting somewhat exasperated.

'Don't you snap at me, clever clogs. I don't think your shot was all that brilliant either,' shouted Gemma in retaliation.

'Stop it both of you, arguing isn't going to help,' intercepted Lorna who at that moment had got the bow completely back to front and somehow wrapped around an arm. 'We need to hurry up or else the witches will be back soon and then we'll all be in big trouble.'

'Yes, sorry,' echoed both Christian and Gemma.

Christian resumed his instructing '. . . and pull back with your right hand, take aim and fire.' Simultaneously, two arrows flew across the room in different directions. One whistled horizontally under the dangling feet of the fairies and embedded itself into the shaft of one of the witches' broomsticks parked on the wall, the other looped straight into the bubbling simmer of the cauldron.

'Oh, just brilliant,' shrieked Christian,

'excellent. We had six arrows between us and now you've just gone and lost two of them before we've even started. I think I should do this,' and he tried to snatch Gemma's bow.

'I am sorry, it's harder to do than you think, it always looks so easy on television,' wailed Gemma, throwing the bow onto the floor in temper.

'Don't be so hard on us, Christian,' Lorna said as she struggled again with the bow and the twine. 'We'll have another go and, after all, we were given these for a reason as you were given the sword for a different reason. Right, now, come on Gem, let's have another go and hope for the best.'

Gemma stopped sobbing and wiped the crocodile tears away with the back of her hand. She picked up the bow and drew another arrow from the sheath. She placed the base of the arrow against the twine and steadied the front against the cane.

'Now, all you have to do is to look at the

target – the peg bats – point the arrow towards one of them, draw back the twine and then fire. Quite simple really!' advised Christian.

Gemma just tutted, deciding to ignore Christian's patronising manner, but followed the instructions.

She jettisoned the arrow with such force that the power of the recoil sent her falling backwards and flat onto the floor. The arrow left the bow, headed towards the ceiling, circled the room above their heads three times and then made straight for the peg bats. The spear of the arrow swooped down to the cobweb and scooped up three of the peg bats by their wings. It headed towards the fire and impaled the bats against the wooden mantelpiece and held them dangling.

'Wow!' exclaimed Christian. 'How did you do that, Gem?'

'Dunno . . . I just dunno,' replied Gemma in a state of shock.

With the noise and draught of the arrow flight, the other three peg bats had started to stir from their drowsy slumber and were beginning to yawn.

'Quick, Lorna, you must do the same before the other bats open their eyes and see what's going on.'

Lorna armed the bow and drew back the twine as quickly as she could in her amateurish way. Yet again, the arrow left the bow, headed towards the ceiling, circled the room above their heads a further three times and made for the remaining three peg bats. It scooped them up and planted them on the mantelpiece next to the other three. Naturally, with all the commotion, all six peg bats were now wide awake and were looking at their new location with much bemusement.

Each one of the fairies had plopped to the ground in a crumpled heap once released from her captor.

'Just look at the state of my dress,' moaned Fern in a vain attempt to brush out the numerous creases.

'Those wretched bats have played havoc with my hair and make up,' remarked Iris as she twisted and prodded her bouffant and patted her cheeks with the palms of her hands.

'Champion, absolutely champion,' yelled Christian to the girls who were also suitably impressed at their handiwork. They all smiled with glee.

CHAPTER 11

The Scarlet Queen's Emporium

The Scarlet Queen was drifting round her circular tower and something was clearly troubling her. 'I smell danger in the air, there's trouble afoot,' she announced in a commanding tone and wagging her index finger in a very menacing fashion. The witches cowered lower when she floated past them – it was obvious that she was angry and they would receive the brunt of her wrath as they happened to be there.

'Bring me the crystal ball,' she ordered. The witches fell over themselves in their haste to oblige. They installed the crystal ball on the imposing granite dais and all four of them took their places around it. The Queen commenced by waving her arms about like the sails of a windmill – clockwise then anticlockwise, creating a swirl of cloud enveloping the company present. In the thick of the smog, she chanted:

'Crystal ball, crystal ball speak to me
what is the meaning of your decree?
Will it be me, or will it be thee?
or will it be children, of which there
are three?'

The smog cleared and the ball came back into view. This time it was completely clear and glowed with a dazzling beam which was almost blinding. The witches averted their gaze, but the Queen stared on, mesmerised, her eyelids widening with the brightness of the glow. In a trance the Queen began muttering words which were incomprehensible, softly at first but they grew louder and louder as she became transfixed to its iridescence. The colours of the crystal ball changed faster and faster and the light became brighter and brighter as the Queen reached her chanting crescendo. Bolts of lightning were shooting out of the ball in all directions. The electric euphoria of the moment was killed by a blood-curdling scream which sent shivers down the spines of the witches.

The Queen fell to her knees in front of the ball. The atmosphere sizzled as the witches waited to see what would happen next. The Queen drew herself up using the dais to steady her, hesitated a minute to regain her composure, then announced, 'The ball tells me a tale, a tale of conflict, a tale of bloodshed, a tale where there is only one winner.' Again wagging her spiny fingers in the air, she paused in contemplation as she held the last word in her breath. 'There will be a battle, this very night, the Angel Children are close . . .'

'How close?' enquired Pandora.

'I don't know at the moment. I have only seen their faces in the ball, but I think they are near as the vision is clear. I must consult the planchette, clear the dais for me, Witch ... move it!' she ordered.

Esmerelda scurried from her perch and removed the crystal ball from the surface to reveal a configuration of scarlet and white runes carved into the granite in a circular arrangement. The Queen took the ruby clasp from her waist strap and placed it carefully in the very centre of the dais and paused. She closed her eyes, turned her head uppermost to face the psyche-delic glass atrium towering above them and commenced ...

'Oh spirit of satanic birth
I look to you to prove my worth,
To show the Queendom belongs to me
And that this world will ne'er be free.'

The witches looked on as the Queen's index finger rested on the edge of the ruby and, motionless, they waited. A twitch in the Queen's finger started the process. The ruby glided toward the first scarlet rune – ⌘, then onto the next ♏, then the next ♋ and so on to spell out the following words ⊠ ⚵ &; ♦ ♒ ◆ ♏ ♏ ❖ ♏ all in scarlet hieroglyphics. 'Excellent,' she exclaimed, 'my power is not diminished,' (we know that's not very good English, but as a Queen, she can speak how she likes). 'I will now proceed to defeat the Angel Children.' She paused in deep thought. 'Children like chocolate,' she mused, 'don't they?' directing her enquiry to the witches. 'What is your potion today?' she asked of them.

'Oh your most Royal Highness, it is a rare delicacy of quite pungent cuisine, a formidable cacophony of flavours, an enlightening array of ingredients – a positive cornucopia for the senses!' waxed Pandora [Chief Cauldron Cook].

'How delightful, what will it do to the children?' asked the Queen.

'It will take their hearts and minds and send them into a state of rare elation. They will sing and dance with Satan and walk backwards through fire until they reach their untimely deaths . . .'

'Oh how wonderful,' burst out the Queen with an unnerving and clearly uncharacteristic display of glee. 'I take it you have mixed it well to taste of chocolate, but make sure that they don't suspect anything else is in it,' she continued, waving her enormous, elongated red painted finger nails in the air.

'Absolutely, absolutely,' echoed the witches.

'Off you go and make preparation for deaths,' ordered the Queen.

The three witches scurried out of the Emporium, very excited about their mission.

The Queen sank to her knees at the foot

of the dais and continued her muttering chant.

CHAPTER 12

Back In The Witches' Cavern

The witches did not know what to make of the sight they saw as they returned to their cavern. The fairies were no longer hanging on the cobweb and they were confronted by three creatures which looked like them, but obviously weren't them.

'Crikey!' shrieked Giselle. 'Who are you?'

'I beg your pardon?' replied Lorna.

With instant recoil, Christian quizzed, 'More to the point, who are you?'

Slightly taken aback by the impertinence of their impostors, Giselle boldly replied, 'We are the Honourable Witches of the Third Order of The Scarlet Queen.'

'What happened to the first Two Orders?' chuckled Christian.

'The cheek of the boy ... but not for long,' scoffed Pandora under her breath.

Without a moment's hesitation and with monumental bravery Lorna intercepted, 'We are the Angel Children and have come to rescue Santa Claus's fairies and over-throw the Scarlet Queen!' Lorna's stomach jumped at the thought of the courage it had taken to say such an important thing in such a delicate situation.

'Why, might I ask, are you wearing our clothes?' asked Esmerelda.

'As I had said to the fairies before, that's a long story but frankly none of your business,' announced Christian. Gemma gulped at the words and cringed when she thought of what might happen to them if they antagonised the witches too much. The witches looked at the six fairies in their coloured dresses sitting waiting patiently along the wall as far away from the real witches as possible.

The witches were actually antagonised at the comment, however they remembered the plan that the Queen had set in place for them to follow. Esmerelda swallowed her annoyance and announced, 'Her Most Royal Highness, The Scarlet Queen, Ruler of Outlands has asked that we make you feel most welcome and ensure that your stay in her Queendom is one of the most amazing experiences you could have endured.'

Pandora coughed slightly and hurriedly corrected Esmerelda, saying *'Enjoyed*, you mean *enjoyed.'*

'Of course, *enjoyed, enjoyed.'* Esmerelda continued, 'You must be very hungry after your long journey and we hear that Angel Children like chocolate. Here's some we prepared for you earlier,' and the witches opened a very ornate box containing the chocolate and offered the contents to the children. Naturally, the children had heard about what happens when you accept sweets from strangers and had been told quite clearly by their mother not to do it, but they helped themselves to a piece each in order not to look impolite. However, whilst they were doing so, they nudged each other with their elbows and pretended to put the chocolate in their mouths. Both Lorna and Christian managed to miss their mouths and secrete the chocolate down the neck of their robes, but Gemma's fell to the floor in front of them all. Dread ran across the children's faces as all of them, including the witches, saw the deceit.

'You ungrateful child,' shouted Pandora. 'That was made from one of my finest recipes – how dare you . . .?'

Gemma trembled as Pandora strutted towards her.

'Don't you touch her, you horrible old bag,' shouted Christian, but Pandora had got hold of Gemma's cassock at the shoulder and began to pull her towards the cauldron.

'Get off her or I'll ...' cried Lorna in desperation. However, quick as a flash, Christian had drawn his sword and was wielding it around the heads of his sisters. With his shield positioned in front of his chest, he lunged forward at Pandora and sliced the blade at her. 'Take that,' he cried in true musketeer style, missing the witch completely and bedding the sword firmly into the wood of a nearby post. It was stuck and everybody gasped. In sheer desperation, Christian swung round yet again and with unbelievable force, walloped Pandora on her back with his shield, sending her floundering across the floor. She let go of Gemma in the process, who reeled as she got back on her feet.

'Nice job,' shouted Lorna, smacking her hands together, only to turn round to encounter the other two witches launching themselves towards them. By this time, the fairies had decided to join in. Now it wasn't the sort of activity they were used to, however they thought they'd better have a go. Petal jumped on the back of Giselle and covered her eyes, whilst Iris grabbed a leg and Buttercup, an arm. Giselle started recounting curses, but the other fairies running around had disorientated her and she too fell to the ground. Swiftly, Christian bashed her on the head with the shield. Whilst the action continued, Gemma was busily pushing pieces of chocolate into the fallen witches' mouths, taking great care to wipe her hands on her robes after each insertion (because she didn't want to catch any germs). As the third witch was dispatched in a similar way by the efforts of Poppy, Fern and Bluebell, the three children stood back and looked at their handiwork. Sadly, the fairies' dresses were in an awful mess, but they had now resigned themselves to the fact that there was nothing more they could do about it.

As they looked on, the witches started to flinch as the chocolate was starting to take effect. They began to display beaming smiles and vacant-looking eyes. They got up and started to dance (backwards, of course as it was the way they did things in Volcanus) and sing, strutting around the cavern, obviously very happy and content in their own little worlds.

Christian managed to lever his sword out of the wood and replaced it in its sheath, then the children and the fairies walked out of the door and left the witches to it.

CHAPTER 13

The Runes

They all crept quietly along the dimly lit passageway, staying in the shadows as much as they could. They seemed to walk for a very long time before they came to any kind of change in the corridor and when they did, it was quite noticeable. A solid iron door, framed with two bright-red burning torches on either side, greeted them. On the stone flag beneath dozed the brown-coloured dragon mentioned to them by Woody. Its face was all covered in scars and as it lay there it lazily brushed its huge, taloned claws over its jaw in a half-hearted manner. The company all fell back into the shadows to decide what to do.

'That's Cassius,' exclaimed Gemma.

'Erm, yes,' replied Lorna.

'Thought so,' nodded Gemma knowledgeably.

'Shush!' cried Christian. 'Don't wake him. You stay here,' he ordered the fairies, 'whilst we go in.'

Now their hearts were really in their mouths.

Christian boldly marched forward, closely followed by his sisters. Cassius, the 13-foot-long fire-breathing dragon, opened an eye and looked up at them. They didn't even need to speak as the dragon just ran his tongue around his mouth, smouldering smoke puffed out of his nostrils and he went back to his sleep.

'Phew, that was surprisingly easy,' whispered Christian.

'He must have thought we were the real

witches,' replied Lorna and Gemma nodded in agreement. They very carefully strode over the dragon's form before they tapped hard on the door.

A very loud 'Enter!' rang out and the children dutifully obeyed.

'Remember, keep your hands and faces covered, so she won't know we're not the real witches,' urged Christian. Terrified, they moved into the Emporium and the Queen beckoned them to her.

'I sense the Angel Children are near, in fact,' she repeated, 'very, very near. I trust the chocolate is ready?' Terrified, the children nodded simultaneously (it was lucky that the witches didn't often speak to the Queen, so it was not unusual for her to receive a simple response – which was a relief for the children).

'To the planchette,' she bellowed. Now this was a problem for the children as they didn't know what a planchette was. However, they got the drift when the Queen moved towards the dais and placed her ruby clasp on the surface. They hesitantly drew nearer and looked on in silence. The Queen started chanting in a language they didn't understand and the ruby beneath her finger moved towards the white rune ♑ and rested on it.

'She's not recognised us,' whispered Christian.

'Shush,' cried Lorna, 'she will if you keep on.'

The Queen looked concerned. The ruby moved towards the second white rune – ♐ – and still it meant nothing. The third white rune gave her the greatest clue – ⊠ ♎⚷. 'Aaah,' she cried, 'this can't be true,' as she tried to remove the ruby from the dais. It would not leave the chart and held her finger to it as it continued on ⚷ ♋ ♎ then ♏ and finally ✦⚷. This time they were all white runes. The ruby came to rest again in the centre of the dais. She screamed so loudly that the whole of the atrium shook, the glass rattled and the children shuddered. Still with her eyes upwards she shrieked 'GABRIEL ...' The children trembled in their sandals.

'This cannot be true, don't lie to me, rune board. I am The Scarlet Queen, the *only* Ruler of Outlands, there can be no other.' Volcanus shook with her outburst and the children quivered in mortal fear. They daren't move a muscle as the Queen was well and truly angry.

'Gabriel must be here and is working his way back into my Queendom,' she announced. 'He is using the Angel Children to assist him. This has gone further than I imagined. I captured the fairies to stop Santa Claus, but I had no idea that Gabriel would also return and harness the support of the Angel Children. My plan is thwarted,' and she hammered her fist on the rune board which sent an almighty blast of fire through the whole of the Queendom.

Her wrath made the earth tremor

beneath the feet of all her subjects and as they stared at Volcanus, the flaming fires in the turrets rose higher and higher and made the entire sky glow red and yellow with rage. The fires all around Volcanus showered red sparks into the air which fell to the ground like molten tinder.

'We must find the Angel Children and kill them,' shouted the Queen in a blinding rage to the children. She scooped up her ruby. 'Leave my presence and do not return until you bring the Angel Children's dead bodies to me,' she ordered and swept out of the room like a whirlwind. She left the children in stunned silence. They were mightily thankful that the Queen hadn't recognised that they weren't the real witches or else they would have been dead already!

'Cripes ...' Christian breathed a long drawn-out sigh. 'What do we do now?'

'I have absolutely no idea,' replied Lorna, looking extremely worried.

'It's the ruby – the ruby,' repeated

Gemma. 'If the Queen doesn't have the ruby, then she doesn't have the power.'

'Oh yes, of course, we'd forgotten about that,' confirmed Lorna.

'Simple solution, just a difficult problem ...' mused Christian.

'Well for starters, we'd better get ourselves out of here because if she does come back, we will be in big trouble,' reflected Lorna.

Outside the door, the fairies were waiting for them and they all made their way back to the witches' cavern.

CHAPTER 14

Gabriel

Returning to the cavern, they found the witches had stopped dancing around the room and were now slumped over the edge of the cauldron, completely spaced out and in their own world. 'Shouldn't hear a peep out of them for a while,' announced Christian.

'How are we going to get the ruby?' asked Gemma.

'I don't know,' replied Lorna sighing heavily.

As they stood, a soft cold whoosh encircled them. The fairies had experienced this before and again, as the current gained momentum, it hooped up like a vortex in front of them. Ahead stood the white apparition, a male form with long straight grey hair and an elongated, straight grey beard triangularly pointed to his toes. The children noticed the large ornate crucifix encrusted with sparkling stones and jewels resting on his chest.

'Permit me to introduce myself, I am Gabriel, Father of All Angels,' he said. 'I am at last honoured to meet you, Angel Children.'

Hesitantly they chorused, 'Honoured to meet you too,' but secretly they were quite nervous at the awesome sight before them.

'No need to ask why you are dressed as witches,' smiled Gabriel. 'I expect that you have got good reason.' In fact, the children had got so embroiled in their replacement personas that they had almost forgotten what they were wearing!

'It's a long story . . .' started Christian.

'And not one you need to go into again

Christian, thank you,' finished Lorna (obviously bored with him repeating the story).

'Please listen, Angel Children,' asked Gabriel.

'Yes, yes of course,' confirmed Lorna.

Gabriel continued, 'Now you are here in Volcanus, and you have met the Scarlet Queen, you must complete the task in hand and take it to its ultimate end.'

'Aaaah, you see, that's where we have got a bit stuck,' informed Christian.

'Just a bit stuck? I would say a lot stuck, to be honest,' added Gemma.

'We haven't worked out how to get the ruby from the Queen and also, we don't have the equipment to tackle the might of the Queen,' added Lorna.

'It is less difficult than you think, our mere presence is your greatest weapon. You are the blessed Angel Children and I am your Leader. Together we can conquer the evil, vest your trust and faith in who you are and what you stand for,' Gabriel heralded.

The children were quite unclear about the sentiment of Gabriel's speech and remained puzzled.

Gabriel continued, 'You must be aware that the power of the Queen is already receding.'

'How do you know that?' asked Gemma quizzically.

'Because she read my name in the runes when you were there, didn't she? Besides which, if the Scarlet Queen still possessed her full powers, she would have known that it was not her own witches in the Emporium and that the impostors were yourselves. She is losing the strength and you are gaining it. This is the start of the end, but you must take care as to how you bring this to its final conclusion,' he halted. 'Now my friends I must leave you to carry out your mission. I know you will do the right thing and make the right decision. We have our roles to play. You must do yours and I must do mine.' With a blink of the eye, Gabriel had vanished.

In the meantime, the fairies had been busy making sure that the real witches weren't going anywhere and had proceeded to tie them to the cobweb from which the fairies had been hanging earlier.

'If that is the case and the witches' power is fading, we could enlist the help of the people of Outlands. We should go back and visit Woody and Flora as we need to rally some support,' suggested Christian.

'Good idea,' agreed Lorna. 'As we have still got our disguises, we shouldn't have too much trouble in moving about Volcanus without drawing too much attention to ourselves.'

So the three of them, plus the fairies, made their way out of the cavern and back to where they had come in. When they ventured into the corridor the children noticed that the air around them was somewhat colder and they shuddered slightly as the chill touched their faces. They instantly drew their hats further down over their eyes, also remembering that they still needed to be undercover. Yet again they stealthily crept in the shadows, hardly daring to breathe in case they gave themselves away. They passed a few dwarves walking backwards and just nodded their heads in acknowledgement, but did not utter a sound. As they crossed the quadrangle their steps quickened, as they felt very exposed without the safety of the corridors. Gemma slid a little as she sensed a thin film of ice had developed beneath her feet as they scurried across the cobbles. The air was definitely colder and they could feel the coolness brush against their noses.

They ran to the safety of the laundry and were greeted by not only Woody and Flora but also a number of rather shabbily dressed goblins who had joined the gathering. The children looked in amazement at the company present. Woody and Flora were not surprised to see the children return and greeted them with, 'We thought yud be back, change is afoot. Word is that the Queen is losing her power.' The fairies had not met Woody and Flora before so they briefly introduced themselves and settled down cross-legged at the back of the meeting. All hope of salvaging their crumpled dresses had now gone.

'The Queen is losin' 'er power,' announced Woody at the front of the gathering. 'The air is getting colder and frost is forming, the season is a changing, and winter is a comin' back again.'

'*She'll* be startin' to get cold now,' added Flora.

'Gabriel must be 'ere. Now is our time to strike!' cried Woody, and he banged his fist firmly on the table.

'Hear, hear,' echoed those present, including the children and the fairies.

(Indeed, unbeknown to her subjects, the Queen had retreated to her bedchamber to fetch her scarlet and black full-length, hooded fur cape before she returned to her Emporium to plan her next move. It was such a long time since she had been cold that she couldn't remember where she had put her scarlet gloves made out of rabbit fur.)

'Aye, the fires round them turrets ain't as high and ferocious as they was and they seems to be subsiding,' added Woody.

'Tis time for you to make your ultimate onslaught . . .' he announced.

CHAPTER 15

The Meeting of the Scarlet Queen and Gabriel

The Scarlet Queen stood over the rune board with her hands held upwards towards the atrium. 'Tell me this is not so,' she wailed. 'My power is ultimate, tell me Gabriel is not back.' At that moment an icy blast flew through the room, around her, beside her, above her. The hooped vortex (which we are now familiar with) appeared in front of her. She recognised the white apparition even before it appeared before her as its male form.

'I have been expecting you,' she announced.

'You should have always been expecting me,' replied Gabriel. 'I said I would return and so here I am. You know you had no right to take my power, my Kingdom and my subjects – you will pay the price.'

'Huh,' huffed the Queen. 'If you think that you, those silly children and those motley fairies stand any chance of over-throwing me, seizing my power and taking my Queendom, then think again Gabriel,' she replied in a disparaging tone.

'Your power is already diminishing. You know that, your people know that and the runes tell you so,' said Gabriel.

'The runes lie,' shouted the Queen.

'No, the runes don't lie. You know that better than I do,' replied Gabriel.

'The runes only tell me this because you have arrived back in my Queendom, not because it is what will happen in the future. This is just a passing visit for you, Gabriel, a vain attempt to regain your power. Your followers are not mighty enough to challenge my authority and you should give up now while you can walk away with your pride,' she said, waving her arms in the air and then recoiling them back to her chest with the cold.

'Oh no, Madam, not this time, this time it shall be to the bitter end. My loyal followers have faith that my legacy will live on, you must trust that the good will out,' Gabriel replied.

'I place my trust only where it belongs and that is with the Exemplar Host of the Scarlet Satanic Order. We won the Battle between Good and Evil, remember.'

'You may well have won the Battle, madam, but it is I who shall win the War. Place your loyalty where you think it lies, madam,' replied Gabriel, 'but you will no longer be his servant. His use for you will diminish as fast as your power. You have served your purpose.'

'Rubbish,' laughed the Queen. 'What gives you the right to speak for the Host of the Scarlet Satanic Order?'

'It is written, madam, in the Holy Order of the Ignatius Prophesy that you will be consumed by your own fires and hell will freeze over.'

'Ughh,' choked the Queen as she toppled sideways with the force of the harsh, cold words. Clinging to the edge of the rune board she staggered toward Gabriel in anger. Gabriel turned his back to the Queen and started to walk away.

'You think you know it all,' shouted the Queen. 'I will show you who has the last word,' she cracked.

As Gabriel walked from her, the Queen grabbed her ruby waist clasp and faced it towards him. 'You will see what I mean Gabriel,' she cried. 'Ad infinitum the Host of the Scarlet Satanic Order!' A bolt of lightning ran jagged from the ruby and struck Gabriel in the centre of his back. Instantly he fell to the floor and in seconds a beacon of fire incinerated his body and Gabriel was no more than a handful of icy glitter on the floor.

'Ha ha!' cried the Queen. 'You see what I mean, Gabriel. No-one doubts my prowess now.' She pulled herself up against the dais and was able to stand upright again. The Emporium was now bitterly cold and she pulled her cloak closer to her skinny frame.

'Now for those stupid children and those pathetic fairies. I must find the witches,' she announced and swept out of the Emporium. She burst through the door of the cavern and a shock wave reverberated through the walls.

'Witches, where are you?' shouted the Queen. 'Where are you?' she anxiously repeated.

'Burp ...' resounded from above.

The Queen looked up and gasped with horror.

'Burp ... oh hello Queenie,' came the voice from above.

'What have you done with my witches?' shrieked the Queen.

'Ah, that was a great meal,' replied Spits,

nonchalantly spitting out a load of sticky froth and ejecting a witch's foot in the process. 'That bit was very smelly,' Spits continued.

In a blinding rage the Queen said, 'You stupid spider. What have you done you useless, senseless, spineless, cretinous lump of arachnid?'

'Hisssss . . .' uttered Spits.

'Just remember, that was your final meal,' the Queen cried and dispatched Spits to a block of wood. 'I will burn you later . . .'

Once again the Queen started to stagger and lose her balance as she attempted to hurry to the quadrangle. The ground was glistening with ice and the air around was white with the falling flakes, with pure sparkling crystals of snow. She slipped as she tried to move forward. 'Where are those children?' she screamed to the palace dwarves as they scurried in every direction with no real idea what they were looking for. They ran round purposelessly as she waved her arms around in outrage. 'I know who those traitors are,' she hollered at the top of her voice as she stumbled towards the laundry. 'Blockhead ... Washy, get yourselves out here. I want a word with you ...' No-one in the laundry stirred. When the Queen got there, the laundry was empty.

CHAPTER 16

The Final Onslaught

Outside Volcanus the snow was also falling fast and gathering as a rich, thick carpet on the floor. It swirled around Woody, Flora, the children, the fairies and goblins. By now, a very strange array of animals had also joined them on the hillside. The numbers had increased as word had got around and now most of the occupants of Rohan were assembled in eager anticipation.

'Is you ready children?' asked Woody.

'Yes we are,' replied Christian, drawing a sharp intake of breath. Beneath their witches' cloaks, they checked their arms –

both Lorna and Gemma carried their small cane bow and sheath, now containing the remaining wooden arrow each had left, and Christian, his sword and shield.

'Good luck my friends,' said Woody as the gathering watched the children make their way down the path and back to Volcanus.

The falling snow quickly covered their tracks and soon the hillside behind them was out of view and shrouded in a blanket of ashen cloud. They carried on, guided by the red illumination of Volcanus's fires before them. As they walked, they noticed that the fires from the turrets were not now blazing as strongly as they had been when they first arrived at the palace. Yet not a whisper passed their lips as they approached the final stage of their quest.

They sneaked up to the slatted bridge and on into the unguarded austere fortress. An eerie silence met them as they made their way into the quadrangle. Against the backdrop of beautiful whiteness, the scarlet silhouette of the towering Queen greeted them.

'Welcome to my palace, once more I may say, Angel Children. Your disguises fool me no more,' said the Queen as she tried to remain composed. 'So this is the final act. Who shall win, I wonder . . .? By the way my dears, Gabriel, Father of All Angels, immortal of all mortals, is dead.'

The children winced with the pain of the words, but said nothing, just trembled even more with fear. 'I had thought what you might look like – pretty little thing,' she said pointing towards Gemma. Gemma shrank back and scowled at the words.

'Well how shall we do this?' questioned the Queen. 'Who shall I kill first? The pretty little thing, her clever elder sister or her heroic brother . . .? Um, ah'. As though drunk with alcohol, the Queen lunged forward towards Gemma.

'Leave her alone,' shouted Christian as he drew his sword from its sheath and held it to his side.

'Quite the little warrior, aren't we?' the Queen mocked. Christian said nothing. 'Let's see what you are made of then, young crusader,' urged the Queen as she removed her waist clasp and flashed the ruby at Christian. The jet of lightning flew across towards Christian but he held his shield in front of him. To their amazement, the jet ricocheted off the shield and struck a pillar beside the Queen. It crashed down sending masonry and dust all around them. The Queen was clearly taken aback (in fact, so were the children).

'Ah, so there's more to you than I thought,' cried the Queen as she raised her ruby and directed it at Gemma. Christian lurched sideways with his shield, but he did not have enough time to reach her and the second lightning jet struck Gemma right in the chest. It smouldered on impact and Gemma slithered to the ground. Both Christian and Lorna were horrified.

'You've killed her, you wicked woman!' screamed Lorna as she ran towards the Queen. Christian pulled her back as the Queen delivered the third jet of lightning which hit Lorna in the leg and she also buckled to the floor next to Gemma.

'Now see who has the power ... courageous Trojan,' scoffed the Queen. Christian was raging as the Queen released a barrage of lightning which bounced all around the quadrangle. The gargoyles dropped from the walls and shattered in splinters, emitting screams as they plummeted; flames ignited much of the brickwork; thunder crashed over their heads and the sky turned blood red. Christian ducked, dived and dodged the rain of lightning from the ruby as the Queen spun round firing it in all directions. The thunderous noise was overwhelming and the atmosphere electric. Christian scurried about to avoid the walls as they fell and the fires that raged around him.

Suddenly the noise was broken by a piercing scream ... the Queen had gone down. Christian raised his eyes, indeed the Queen was on her knees and shouting towards the blood-red sky. He did not understand what she was saying as she was pulling at the arrow sticking out from her heel. She saw Christian staring at her. 'It's not over yet,' she cried from her faltering position, and issued the fiercest strike of lightning Christian had ever seen. He had no time to position his shield in defence and it hit him in the arm with such force that it pelted him backwards and he struck his head against one of the remaining pillars. Yet again the Queen let out another blood-curdling scream. The Queen now had an arrow sticking out of her stomach where the ruby waist clasp would have been positioned. Lorna's face was distraught as she stooped in horror at her actions. She fainted. The Queen started to crawl across the ground towards Lorna, overcome with pain and rage. She dragged herself to where Lorna lay and raised her half torso to deliver a blow with her hand holding the ruby.

'Aaaaaaaahhhhh!' screeched the Queen. 'You ... you ...' and she fell back down to the ground. Christian stood over her, his hand still holding the shaft of the sword with the blade firmly embedded in the heart of the Queen. The Queen lay motionless. A trail of black blood trickled across the pure white snow. The whole world went silent.

Christian was in a daze when Woody shouted, 'Get the ruby, grab the thing.' Christian snapped out of his trance and reached to the Queen's hand. The ruby was firmly held in her grasp and he had to peel back each of her gripping fingers to release the stone. He tugged his sword out of her body and started to walk away. Behind him, a tremendous cracking noise broke the silence. The ground beneath the Queen had split open and widened to a crevice. She was pulled down into the boiling, black abyss below. Her screams could be heard throughout every inch of Outlands.

Christian was dumbstruck with horror, but Woody grabbed the shoulder of his cassock and wrenched him from the scene. 'We've got to get out o' here pretty quick,' he hollered, 'or we'll be surrounded by fire and down where she is if we're not careful.'

'No, no,' cried Christian. 'There's Lorna and Gemma.'

'Ay dunno fret yourself,' said Woody guardedly, 'we've got 'em, just shush and 'urry.' Christian carefully placed the stone in his purse belt and they skated on the ice as they ran out of the palace. When they had got over the drawbridge to safety on the other side they paused to catch their breath.

Although he could hardly speak, Christian managed to utter. 'But you, you ... ran forwards ...?'

Woody gave a wry grin and said to Christian, 'You 'ave slain the Queen. The Queen's curse binds us no longer. See the seasons have returned, we are now in the thick of winter, the snow is falling, the air is fresh and the people are free.' Woody raised his arms to the sky and spun round, jumping with excitement. 'Gabriel has returned and has saved us,' he cried with pure joy.

Christian gulped and took courage to say, 'No, Woody, Gabriel is dead. The Queen killed him, she said so,' he stammered. Woody said nothing. Christian could feel no such elation as he recalled the plight of his sisters and trudged through the heavy snow behind Woody. He stooped to wipe the Queen's black blood from his sword in the snow. He was exhausted, cold and dispirited as Woody led him back to the assembled crowd who were laughing, singing and dancing, rapturously greeting their hero back to the fold.

Deflated, Christian made his way to Woody's cart only to see two smiles he immediately recognised. They were those of his sisters. 'But, but ... you are burnt,' stammered Christian to Lorna, and turning to Gemma, 'and you are ... dead! Yes, dead,' in total disbelief. They both chuckled at Christian and looked at Woody.

'Never presume owt in this world,' laughed Woody, 'the jet of lightning struck Gemma's crucifix which was protecting 'er 'an when you took the ruby, the injury to both Lorna and you were instantly healed.' Christian felt his arm where the lightning had struck and there was no sign of what had happened, nor the knock to his head.

'Quick, look!' shouted Gemma, pointing to Volcanus. Whilst they had been distracted with the reunion, Volcanus was now burning ferociously, the flames leaping higher and higher towards the sky which was now all scarlet red against the deep blackness of the night. As the gathering looked on, the heat towards them got more and more intense even though they were standing in the cold, knee-deep blanket of fluffy white snow. As they viewed the scene, an enormous explosion rang through Outlands rocking the earth from its core. The tremor shook the hill on which they were huddled and as they watched in the distance, Volcanus descended down into the volcanic crater which had been its foundation. Black molten lava blew forth from the crevice and spouted into the sky above. The red fires were no longer.

'The *Royal Puritan Decree, The Queen's Command*, as been broken,' announced Woody with great zeal.

'*I will return . . .*' thundered through the skies, followed by a spine-chilling laugh which vibrated through the hill on which they were perched. At the same time, a huge bellow echoed around them and Cassius the 13-foot dragon flew out of the epicentre of the volcano and vanished into the black clouds above.

Nothing happened for a few moments, until the cloud cleared and the sun rose behind Volcanus, the snow stopped falling, the sky turned blue and a feeling of calm, peace and tranquillity enveloped them all.

CHAPTER 17

The Final Act

'I'll get you back to the edge of the wood and we'll meet up with Art an' 'e'll tek you back to meet up with Haggis,' confirmed Woody. 'I suggest that you tek your witches' smocks off now, or you'll be in trouble.' They smiled and disrobed, leaving the outfits and hats on Woody's cart. The journey passed much more uneventfully than the one which had brought them. The children and the fairies were very thoughtful as they pondered their adventure whilst trudging through the powdery snow. As Woody had said, Art was waiting for them at the edge of the wood with a beaming grin on his face.

'Angel Children, you have shown immense courage and determination and it is my absolute honour to escort you back to the Kingdom of Heaven,' announced Art proudly. With these words each child thanked and hugged Woody and with a small tear in the girls' eyes, they bade him farewell.

In very little time they had returned to Art's hut. In complete contrast to their previous visit, Esther, Erin and Aron were enjoying the frivolity and excitement of the season. Festive holly adorned the walls, jolly music played from the tiny gramophone and a beautifully decorated Christmas tree glistened with tinsel, lights and baubles in the corner of the scullery.

'Oh welcome, welcome my children,' gushed Esther. 'We are so pleased to have you in our company, you must join us for dinner. I have simply been cooking as fast as I can ready for your arrival. Come to the fireside and warm yourselves.' The children and the fairies were quite over-whelmed by all the attention they were receiving and placed themselves in a row with their backs to the inviting, roaring warmth of the glow.

The gathering enjoyed the most wonder-ful feast they had ever seen – turkey with stuffing, cranberry sauce, roast potatoes, fresh green vegetables and rich brown gravy followed by a flaming Christmas pudding and ice cream, all washed down with mugs of ginger beer. The meal over, the fairies started the dancing to Aron playing enchanting tunes on his Irish fiddle. A rather loud rap on the door halted the enjoyment and slowly Art opened the door.

A blast of chilled snowy froth swirled round the scullery and, 'Ho, ho, ho!' broke the silence as Santa Claus entered the scullery, followed by Haggis. The whole company was delighted. 'Can't stop, busy night,' laughed Santa Claus as he handed out presents to Erin and Aron, Esther and Art. 'Must go, Merry Christmas to you all. Thank you so much Angel Children,' and within a moment he had whistled out as fast as he had come in. The fairies of course followed. Erin had been given the prettiest doll the child had ever seen, Aron had received a wooden train set, Esther had got an exquisite lace tablecloth and Art, the finest chisel set he had ever laid eyes on.

'The *Royal Puritan Decree, The Queen's Command* is no longer,' announced Art as he raised his tankard full of ale to all at the party.

They all cheered 'Hurray!'

The entertainment continued for some time after Santa had left, until Haggis announced that they must return to the Grotto to make their final journey home. Despite the rapturous welcome they had received, Gemma was a little sad because she had felt in her purse belt and couldn't find the pure white feather that she had found in Santa's Grotto on her first visit on her own. It must have dropped out whilst she was dancing with Erin and Aron, but she couldn't see it anywhere. With very fond wishes and much hugging, the trio bade farewell and left the family to savour the magic moments of their Christmas.

Following Haggis, the children ventured out into the crisp, chill December night. The scene was breathtaking. The tall, conical pine trees were snow laden. Crystal icicles hung from their fronds and sparkled like vertical diamonds against the moonlit sky. A cold blast of air swirled around them and the children looked towards the moon. Their eyes sparkled as the vision before them was awesome and quite overwhelming. Against the shining of the bright moon emerged a silhouette, first the shape of a horse, then a spiral gold horn shone, then the shape of a person astride the horse.

As the vision became clearer, Lorna blurted out, 'It's Nadir, ruler of the empire of Zenith.'

'And look,' confirmed Christian, 'it's Gabriel on his back.' Christian clutched his purse belt, remembering that he still had the ruby. He carefully drew it from its haven and held it up. As he rested the stone in his hand, they watched as its colour turned from red, to pink, to white, and lit up the whole of the world around them. After a couple of seconds, the brightness of the moon faded and Nadir and Gabriel disappeared.

'Nadir has reclaimed his Kingdom and the world will be at peace again,' smiled Haggis.

'Look Haggis,' cried Christian, 'this stone is no longer ruby red, it's white, well, crystal coloured.'

'Aye, thought so,' said Haggis. 'He has turned it back to a diamond now, *Gabriel's diamond*. He needs to have it back, but not just today eh, Christian? He knows it's safe with you!'

'No, not just today,' replied Christian, as he carefully put the diamond back in his purse belt.

The powdery fluff that was the Tall Tree Forest floor glistened as the moon lit their way. The children ran in all directions, frolicking with fun and excitement. They threw snowballs at each other and whooshed the soft flakes up to their faces, making Haggis laugh. The children giggled with happiness. The miserable Christmas tree which had concealed Santa's Grotto when they left had been replaced by the solid cathedral-styled oak door which they had come through. The children ran up to it and sprang the latch to open it. Inside, Santa's Grotto was deserted and all the toys had gone. The eerie silence was strange, but despite that, the children felt comfortable. Haggis handed them over to Morsel who had been waiting for them.

'Job done?' cried Morsel with a knowing grin on his face.

'Yes, I suppose it is,' beamed Christian.

'Well done, oh so well done,' chuckled Morsel.

The children followed Morsel and effort-lessly made their way back up the 998 steps. At the top they paused and thanked Morsel. Gemma yet again had a tear in her eye as they walked back through the under-stairs panel.

The light was on and Uncle Nicholas was still in his study reading so they headed up to bed as they had been away for ages. They fell asleep as soon as their heads touched the pillows.

'Wakey, wakey!' rang out through the landing of the vicarage. 'It's Christmas Day. *We wish you a Merry Christmas, we wish you a Merry Christmas,*' sang Uncle Nicholas.

Lorna was the first to wake up and she sat on the side of the bed, wiping the sleep from her eyes as she looked at her clothing. She was in her warm, thick nightdress and her slippers were beside the dressing table. She felt her nightdress. Gone was the hessian smock, the fawn calico shirt, the trousers and the leather sandals. No sign of the wide belt with the bow and arrows. In fact no hint of any of the adventure they had undertaken was evident whatsoever. No bites from the biting beetles, no marks from the munching mosquitoes and definitely no wound where the Queen had delivered the jet of lightning that hit her in the leg and buckled her to the floor! It was quite the most realistic dream she had ever had. She wasn't going to mention it to the others – they would only laugh at her as she was always the most serious one of them all.

Christian was the only one who seemed to possess any lasting evidence of the adventure which had befallen them as, when he looked at his hand where the fish's fangs had made quite a deep cut, the area had healed but the scars still remained. Christian, however, thought nothing of it, thinking that the scars would fade in time. The three children met each other on the landing, but said nothing other than 'Merry Christmas' between them.

With a mixture of excitement and anticipation, they made their way down the rickety stairs and into the scullery. Betty greeted them with a resounding 'Merry Christmas' and enveloped each of them in a hug by her ample physique. She had already started to prepare a wonderful-smelling Christmas lunch and the kitchen had become a hive of activity. The children had a light breakfast and were then summoned to the study to meet up with Uncle Nicholas before they went to church for the Morning Service.

They were all now slightly nervous,

wondering if they had been good enough to have received a Christmas present. Lorna knocked on the huge wooden door and a voice from within called 'Come in, children.' They walked in single file, Lorna first, followed by Christian and Gemma bringing up the rear. Uncle Nicholas was standing looking towards them as they entered the room with his back to the roaring study fire. He rested his hand on the top of his favourite high-back leather armchair which was facing the fire. He pointed towards the base of the enormous Christmas tree under which lay three small packages. The children picked up one each and sat cross-legged on the floor to open them.

Simultaneously they untied the string, unwrapped the paper covering and found a small box. With apprehension, they took the lids off the boxes and held their breath ... in each of the boxes lay a gold crucifix on a coarse metal chain with a quite large ring. They recognised them immediately and smiled at one another and then at Uncle Nicholas. Only Gemma's box included another small object, a pure white feather, *her* pure white feather which she had lost at Art's house. A million questions ran through their heads, but Uncle Nicholas bade them quiet as he beckoned them towards the fireside. They obeyed and stood next to him. He ushered them round him and towards the front of his leather armchair. The children gasped with delight as they saw their mother seated in the chair with her arms wide to greet them.

It was the most extraordinary Christmas the children had ever had . . .

Printed in the United Kingdom
by Lightning Source UK Ltd.
135106UK00001B/205-246/P